THE GHOST DOG

THE TANESH EMPIRE TRILOGY: BOOK 3

LEAH CUTTER

Tainted Waters

Spoiled Harvest

The Chronicles of Franklin

The Popcorn Thief

The Soul Thief

MAP

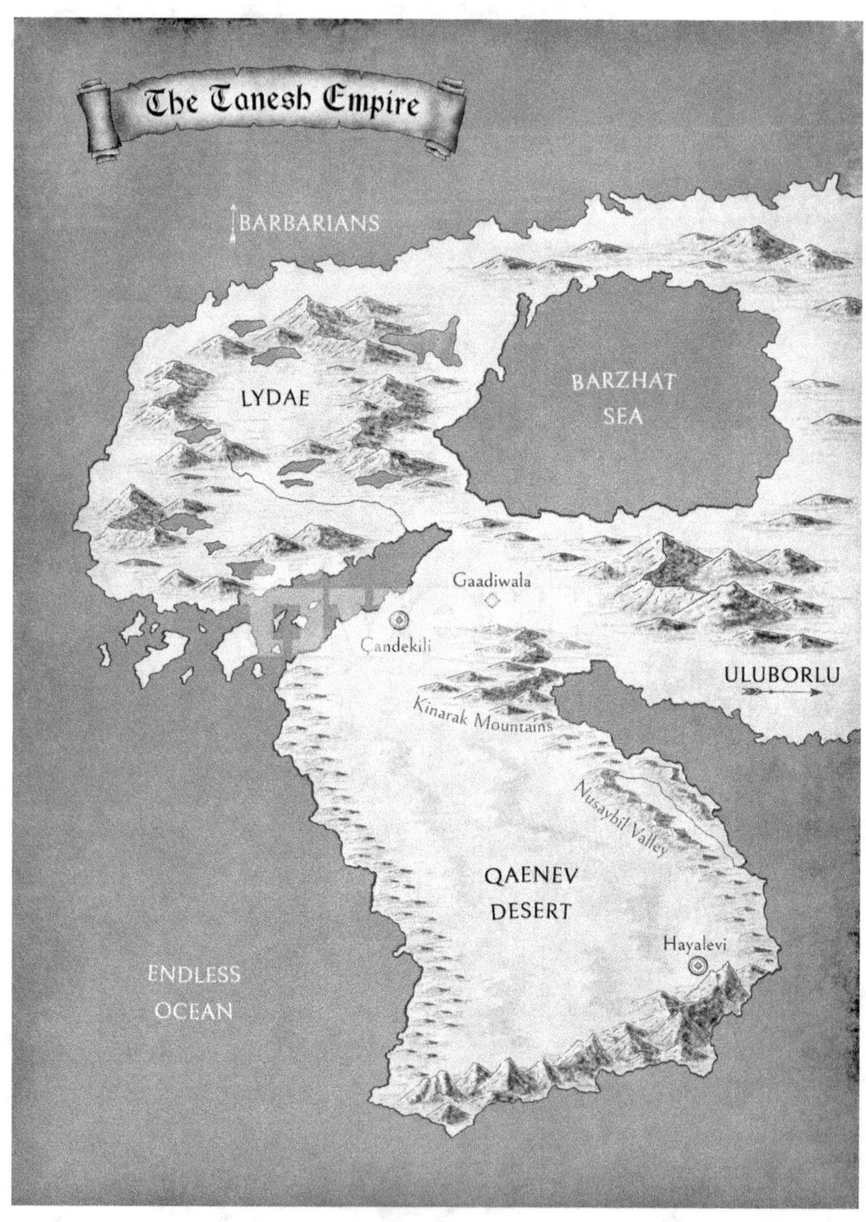

The Tanesh Empire
BARBARIANS
LYDAE
BARZHAT SEA
Gaadiwala
Çandekili
ULUBORLU
Kinarak Mountains
Nusaybil Valley
QAENEV DESERT
Hayalevi
ENDLESS OCEAN

PRONUNCIATION GUIDE

Ç—pronounced as the S in "Sea." TRU-llis (Trulliç)

Zh—pronounced as the S in "Measure." MEER-i-zhah (Myrizhah)

ş—Pronounced as SH. KAR-desh (Kardeş)

ğ—Pronounced with a hard, guttural sound. AH-gkhree-khat (*ağrikat*)

CHAPTER ONE

TRULLIÇ

TRULLIÇ DREAMED OF THE OLD kings. He traveled east across the desert, toward the grand city of Osmerli, the capital of the old kings that the emperor had destroyed over two hundred years before. Hayalevi, the new city that Trulliç had raised, now stood in its place.

Thick walls surrounded Osmerli, eighteen feet tall and three feet wide, made of cold gray granite, quarried from the mountains south of the city. Banners flew over the western city-gate entrance. Trulliç's banner were similar: gold and green stripes against an off-white background. He'd deliberately made his different, however, by adding a black horseshoe to the center, to represent the glass horseshoe that had been created at his birth.

However, in the dream, while his banner flew next to the ones of the old kings, the edges of his were tattered and the horseshoe in the center looked like a broken circle, while the banners of the kings appeared brand new.

The buildings were similar between the two cities: beautiful walls built out of rust-colored stone. Thick, too, in order to keep out the desert heat, or hold in the warmth of a winter fire. Fine lattice work and glass covered the windows. Embroidered gold and green blankets hung in front of the open doorways, every traveler a welcome guest.

Trulliç whirled around the city like a dust devil, visiting each temple.

The buildings were in the same places as the ones he'd raised, though in Osmerli, they were much grander.

The first was the temple dedicated to the goddess Onnet, and had not one but two side courts for dancers and performers. Fine white sand covered the circular performance space, and bleachers carved out of yellow stone surrounded the courts, each able to hold over one hundred people. Though neither court was full at the time, Trulliç still felt a pang of jealousy knowing that his small temple had yet to draw so many followers.

The market square was bursting with merchants selling exotic wares, like carved wood from the land of the Uluborlu far to the east, dried grapes from the kingdom of Lydae to the north, the finest salt from the coastal regions, as well as tapestries, well-made leather goods, finely spun wool, and more. Additional caravans entered the city hourly, their camels piled high with goods, the sheep and goats they drove of the highest quality.

Trulliç knew he just had to be patient. People would come to his city. It would swell with their stories and songs.

He didn't have time, though. Not before the emperor attacked.

But the dream continued, taking him by the cool temple of goddess Enkat who brought the rains, then out to where Xannil greeted the dawn, then circled back to the dark spot where Forit's temple stood.

A simple red ribbon was strung across the entrance to Forit's temple. Strong magic pushed everyone away from the spot. Still, wilted flowers lay at center of the opening, placed there by couples long separated as well as lovers with broken hearts.

Then Trulliç spun outward, to the colorful blue and black temple of the goddess Barzhat who welcomed and judged those who died. A group of star sisters—female illusionists—were camped there, a *kabil* traveling on their way to the *panayirat,* the annual celebration and meeting of the seven star-sister tribes. They practiced throwing knives at man-shaped targets, dummies stuffed with straw. Trulliç didn't look closely enough to see the faces they'd painted on their targets, too afraid that he might see his own there.

Finally, he traveled inward, toward the heart of the city. The smaller temple of Serrat/Serril stood guard there, the two-faced god who inhabited the desert and desolate places, both black and white, the trickster who'd brought magic to mankind.

But the temple was dwarfed by the palace of the kings. While in Hayalevi, Trulliç's tower was easily the biggest building, here in the city of the old kings, it was only the size of *one* of the palace's towers, and there were six of them, three along each side of the palace walls. In between the towers stood huge buildings, gardens, stables, fountains, trees—like a mini-city within the greater city.

Trulliç wondered if he should build a palace just as fine one day. However, he was the only desert magician. Maybe he needed merely a single tower.

Had there been six kings? One for each tower? He couldn't recall any poems that listed their names or how many kings there had been. The history, what little there was of it, merely mentioned that there had been more than one.

All the books about the old kings had been lost when the emperor had destroyed the city, killing the kings and their descendants.

Something tugged Trulliç to the right, as though the dream was responding to his thoughts. Maybe he was missing a truth about the dead kings.

Trulliç gasped as he came around the edge of the building.

Grand steps led up to the entrance of the tower, made out of red tile with geometric designs, diamonds and circles, embossed on the front. Long platforms jutted out from the building on either side of the steps.

Trulliç willed himself to slow, then finally, stop, so he could examine the statues.

A huge dog carved out of stone lay on each platform. Each of the dogs was about the length of three men and the height of two. The dogs' front paws were stretched out in front of it with the hind legs curled at the back, the head upright, the tops of the floppy ears raised, as if listening.

These didn't appear to be just any kind of dog: no, these looked like blood hounds, the beasts conjured by the emperor to escort a pregnant woman who carried a babe of power. They were carved out of cool, white marble, struck through with black.

Trulliç had the uncomfortable feeling that the statues watched him and had judged him unfit to enter.

A rumbling growl erupted as soon as Trulliç set one foot on the stairs. Stubbornly, he brought up his other foot, climbing, daring the dogs to do their worst.

Trulliç shook as the statues began to move, the rock grinding against itself. The noise set his teeth on edge. He took another step, determined to go meet the kings of old, though the stairs now seemed endless, the steps rising forever up to the sky. The smell of the ancient desert, those parts rarely seen by man, washed over him, full of dry baked sand and bleached bones.

One of the marble blood hounds jumped down onto the steps in front of Trulliç. The ground shook under Trulliç's feet. He stopped, startled, his heart pounding.

However, the statue was no longer huge—instead, it had shrunk down to the size of a single man. It shook itself, looking remarkably like a dog shaking sand from its fur, then it started to rise up on its hind legs.

Trulliç gasped. The form of the dog elongated. What was it changing into?

Fog suddenly poured in, hiding the living statue. Trulliç felt himself yanked backwards, traveling rapidly out of the city and over the sands, only to be dumped onto the hard ground, waking with a start.

Trulliç gasped, finding it hard to catch his breath. Fear and horror gibbered in his mind. He shook his head and made himself sit up.

He was still in his tower, the one he'd raised in Hayalevi. The coolness of the night would be stolen by the heat of the day soon, the sky beyond his window already lightening. His room stood mostly empty: a simple chest in the corner to hold his few belongings, a wooden bookshelf that was already collecting ancient books of poetry he'd found at the market, the straw-stuffed pallet he slept on with his sandals beside it. In the corner, the snake-headed staff made by the emperor glowered behind its thick case of glass.

Try as he might, Trulliç couldn't remember the poem that had mentioned how the old kings had once worshipped dogs. He knew there had to be one, as he had such a clear memory of it.

If Trulliç hadn't killed Atça, his old mentor, Trulliç could have asked him. Atça probably would have remembered, as he had a much better mind for that sort of thing than Trulliç. He'd also studied for decades more than Trulliç had.

Riyune stirred against Trulliç's leg.

Trulliç glanced down. He couldn't help but shiver again when he realized just how much the coloring of the stone dogs matched the one laying against his leg.

Once Trulliç and Nadeem had left the cavern in the middle of the desert, Riyune had turned back into a dog, no longer just a ghostly shape with the bones showing, a figure they could see through.

Riyune only appeared to be dead in the land of myths.

However, even in the mid-day sun, Riyune cast a light shadow, as if he were no longer solid. In addition, Riyune had stopped eating and drinking. He still did normal dog things like sit on his butt to scratch at his neck with his hind legs, and he always circled three times before he laid down, as if flattening the area before he slept.

In the dim light of the morning, Trulliç saw Riyune raise his head and stare over his shoulder. Then the dog nodded once, as if saying, *Yes.*

It brought Trulliç back to his original question.

Had the kings of old merely worshiped dogs who happened to resemble blood hounds?

Or did the old kings have the ability to transform into the shape of a dog?

Before the dream had been snatched away, had that been what the figure in front of Trulliç had been changing into? Going from dog to king?

***

It had been two weeks since Trulliç had stopped Marius in the myth lands, two weeks since Riyune had sacrificed himself to close the guard stone, only to return as an almost normal dog. Well, what went for normal when it came to Riyune.

Two weeks since Nadeem had stepped up to the brink of death, welcoming it the same way that the star sisters welcomed the goddess Barzhat, with open arms and love.

Two weeks since Trulliç had realized that he had feelings for the former star sister. Feelings that still confused him.

Feelings that he was certain Nadeem didn't return.

But then again, Nadeem hadn't fully returned to the land of the living, either. She remained distant, as if she'd been encased in cool glass, always looking out but not really there anymore.

That morning, Trulliç found Nadeem in the back kitchen with Myrizhah—his mother—and Seydat—his secretary, for want of a better term, the young woman who kept him organized. The three women worked in a comfortable silence, not bothering each other with questions or inane commentary.

Trulliç had recently realized that everyone in Hayalevi had grown more quiet since coming to his city. It wasn't a somberness that infected his people, but rather, the peace of the desert.

The kitchen was much larger than a single family's hearth: it had a large hand-pump in the far corner for bringing water up into a basin, two iron stoves for cooking, as well as a large fireplace for roasting.

Nadeem stood next to one of the stoves. She broke a piece of dough off the mound in front of her, flattened the piece between her hands, then threw it into a sizzling pan, grilling the flatbread they'd serve that day, both for themselves and to any guests who arrived.

Trulliç levitated a warm piece of flatbread from the pile that Nadeem had finished cooking just before she flopped down the most recently finished piece.

"Hey!" she said. She made to snatch at the piece of bread still floating in mid-air, then turned to glare at Trulliç. "You could wait until I was finished."

"Where's the fun in that?" Trulliç asked, teasing.

He was aware of the sad look Myrizhah shot him. She knew too much of her son's soft heart, and could probably guess the extent of his feelings for Nadeem. As well as the state of Nadeem's hard heart.

Nadeem's glare softened and she rolled her eyes at him before returning to her task. She wore an outfit more like Myrizhah's and Seydat's than like a star sister: a bluish-white blousy shirt the color of a hazy sky, under a green-and-white striped sleeveless tunic that fell to her knees. Unlike the other women, though, Nadeem wore tight black pants made of some sort of stretchy fabric that gave Trulliç far too many ideas about all the muscles in Nadeem's legs.

Though Nadeem was no longer a star sister, she still wore a wide brown-leather belt that held mysterious pouches and the traditional three knives. He was certain that she had other weapons hidden on her body. She'd cropped her dark brown hair even shorter than usual, almost as shorn as a spring sheep. Though he couldn't fault her for it, generally only married women wore their hair long. Both his mother and Seydat wore their hair down past their shoulders, held back by a *chafiyek*, a square scarf that was worn over the crown of the head, but could also be rewrapped over the face and mouth to protect a person from sand and sun.

"Any word yet?" Myrizhah asked, as she did every morning, looking up from the other stove where she was standing. Seydat walked over to the corner and poured fresh water from the basin there into the bowl she was mixing. Trulliç knew that despite how she kept working, she was completely focused on the conversation.

Trulliç sighed and replied to his mother. "None of the caravans have any news of the emperor or troop movements," he said.

"They're coming," Nadeem told him.

"I know that," Trulliç said. He took a deep breath, trying to control his ready rage. He made some progress over the last couple of weeks, but he knew he was missing something, a crucial step to help him get over his anger so it wouldn't get the best of him during the middle of a battle.

Trulliç watched his mother stir a pot that contained a thick chicken soup, flavored with mint and oregano, that would be served to any guests who came that day.

He knew she wasn't to blame for how Atça had treated him. How could she have known? How could anyone other than another magician have understood just how poorly Atça was training Trulliç? Only someone with power would have realized how Atça's lies were twisting Trulliç and his abilities.

Myrizhah had done her best, carrying a newly born babe from the northern part of the Kingdom of Lydae, where he'd been born, all the way back south, through the entire Tanesh Empire, home to Gaadiwala, the village on the edge of the Qaenev desert. The trip had taken her years, and Trulliç had been able to walk as well as talk by the time they'd arrived.

Though Myrizhah rarely spoke of her journey now, he remembered her telling travelers about it at the Horseshoe Tavern that his uncle owned. He knew that she'd edited the tale, only reciting the good parts.

Not the parts that Trulliç remembered: the endless walking, how starved they'd both been at least half the time, how desperately hot and cold it had grown on the road.

No, his mother had done everything she possibly could have to give Trulliç the chance for a good life. She'd come to the desert, gotten Atça to mentor him, raised the money for Trulliç to go to school instead of working like his cousins.

A fine strand of hair slipped out of Myrizhah's *chafiyek*. Shock rocked through Trulliç's body when her realized just how gray his mother had grown. He swallowed against an uncomfortably dry throat.

His mother had always seemed undefeatable to him, a desert rock that withstood torrential spring rains, punishing summer suns, as well as roaring winter storms.

As she pushed her hair back, she seemed to feel his eyes on her. She turned to look at him, the question in her eyes clear: did he need something from her? Anything? Everything?

She was always willing to do whatever she could to help him. Which included smacking him when he most deserved it.

He smiled at her, feeling something loosen in his chest, a band across his heart that he hadn't realized had been there.

Then he shook his head. No, he didn't need anything more from her.

She'd done her best by him. She'd always done her best.

And he could forgive her for Atça.

Trulliç traveled to the northern most part of the Qaenev desert later that morning. Riyune raced at his side, able to keep up despite how Trulliç just *flew* across the sands.

The old Riyune wouldn't have been able to move at such speeds. Admittedly, the dog had never been normal, but since dying in the myth lands, he was even less so now.

Trulliç helped Nadeem as they traveled, loaning her more fleet feet so she could race beside him. She didn't enjoy being carried at great speed, but she accepted his help while she mostly moved on her own.

The pair of them were visiting a village up here, to see if any of the caravans that had come from the north during the last couple of weeks could report on the emperor's troop movements.

Trulliç knew that the emperor was coming. He'd bring a grand army with him, intent on destroying Hayalevi and killing Trulliç. The emperor had already sent his guard, intent on breaking the desert heart free from the myth lands so that the emperor might become a god.

He would usurp the goddess Barzhat. All death would feed him. He'd sup on the souls of those who died, possibly killing them forever.

Barzhat merely judged those who died, giving each a vest with teardrop-shaped weights on it, each weight representing the bad things that a person had done while they were living. Then the person had to dance in the golden court of Barzhat until the weights fell off and the soul could be reborn.

Trulliç had to stop the emperor. He'd sworn a blood oath to protect the land.

He still didn't know how.

Finding out how many troops the emperor intended to bring to the desert at least felt as though he was doing *something*. Discovering which direction the emperor was intending to come on his invasion also seemed to be right.

However, Trulliç had never fought a great battle or commanded troops. He'd read a lot of poems and stories about such battles but he didn't have any experience. Hell, he didn't even really have *guards*. His magic was enough to defend him in the desert.

Trulliç had to stop the emperor and his bid to become a god, as well as to destroy Hayalevi. Somehow. Hopefully without killing anyone, because the emperor would only grow stronger with each death.

The town of Egreliki was inland from the sea, but along the main trade routes. The garrison that the emperor had sent two weeks before wouldn't have passed through the town, as it was south of where they'd first entered the desert. It lay ensconced in the Yerminil peaks, foothills in front of the town protecting it from the desert, while close enough to the Higli mountains to catch the rainfall that came over the mountains.

The town itself had been built close to an oasis, so many of the buildings were actually made of wood, a rarity for desert towns. The normal red brick had been whitewashed, making Egreliki shine in the morning sunlight.

It made Trulliç proud that he had such a beautiful town in his land. He was glad he wore a more formal tunic, striped in gold and green, along with brown pants that Myrizhah had insisted he change into (since they were clean) as well as a new, off-white muslin shirt, and his sturdy leather sandals.

They touched down just at the edge of town, at the base of the foothills, where the land gave way to proper desert. Trulliç wasn't certain why Egreliki was part of his territory, as the heart of the town didn't sit in the desert, but he had no doubt that it was, indeed, his.

He pushed his power down deep under the ground, seeking water and wealth as Nadeem and Riyune waited beside him.

Ah. That was why this town was also his. The water that kept it alive originated in an aquifer that had its toes in the desert. The water rights were his, which meant the town was as well.

Water meant life. Trulliç had always known that. He shook his head as he felt his emotions grow heated.

Atça had been planning on bankrupting the poorer parts of Gaadiwala, in particular, where Trulliç's family lived, just so the magician could make himself more rich.

Trulliç ground his teeth, remembering how ineffective he'd been at stopping the magician at first. How he'd gotten lost under the ground because Atça hadn't given him the right training. How Atça had lied to him all those years.

Nadeem laid a hand on Trulliç's arm, bringing him back to the surface. He threw a grateful smile at her, though shame and fear swam in his belly. He couldn't afford to get lost like that!

Atça was dead. Trulliç had killed his former mentor.

But Atça's death still hadn't been enough. Would never be enough.

Trulliç couldn't do anything about that now, though. Instead, he pasted a smile on his face to greet the small group of people coming down the main path, away from the town and out toward the desert. He needed to at least play the part of a great magician and not a trapped, angry boy.

"Greetings!" called a fair voice.

Trulliç blinked, surprised. He'd assumed the mayor or other official would be there. Not a woman.

Then again, she had the short hair of someone unmarried. Maybe she worked for the mayor? She wore pants like a man, though the color of burnt orange and very baggy. Her blouse was the color of the finest desert sand, golden and rich, while her sleeveless tunic was forest green, with stripes of much lighter greens running down it. Her *chafiyek* was also striped, yellow, red, and orange.

The people behind her were just as colorfully dressed. He knew instinctively that they'd stand out like spring flowers against the white walls of the town. They had the dark skin of the desert people, with dark eyes and hair.

"I am Zehra," the woman said as she led the group forward. "I am the mayor of Egreliki. Welcome to our town! We are happy that you decided to honor us this morning."

Trulliç blinked, surprised. A woman mayor? He glanced for a moment at Nadeem. Well, why not? His mother was certainly capable of running not only a tavern, but an entire city. If she'd stayed in Gaadiwala, she could have easily been in charge of the entire village after Atça had died.

If the men would have let her.

"I am Trulliç," he said belatedly, bowing his head.

Zehra gave him a knowing smile, as if she realized where his thoughts had gone. She was probably used to such judgments by men.

"This is Nadeem, a traveler, and my best friend," Trulliç continued, indicating the woman standing on his right.

She raised her chin and turned her head slightly, so that at least some of the people gathered saw her mangled cheek, where a star sister was usually marked with a star cut into their flesh.

He didn't bother introducing Riyune, though Zehra did give the dog a questioning glance.

"What can I do for the desert magician?" Zehra asked. "Besides provide him with the best hospitality that a town can offer?"

Trulliç smiled. It was a bit forward of her to ask what he needed before offering him hospitality. Then again, that seemed to be her nature.

"I need to talk with any caravans that have recently arrived. Particularly from the north," Trulliç said.

Zehra nodded, her face suddenly serious. "It's the emperor, isn't it?" she asked quietly. "He's coming. With troops."

"How do you know?" Trulliç said, surprised. Most of the towns people he'd talked with, as well as the caravans, had no idea.

The people in Hayalevi knew, though. They shared Trulliç's dreams and fears too often.

Zehra frowned. "I felt you coming to our town," she said. "So I knew to be here to greet you. I've dreamed of the great battle you had with the emperor's guards." She threw a glance at Riyune. "Of your sacrifices." She took a deep breath, then looked at him with unguarded eyes. "All the sacrifices we're going to have to make."

Trulliç blinked. This woman had no magic. She wasn't a star sister. She didn't have power on her own.

But she seemed more sensitive than most, and the tragedy her eyes held tore at Trulliç's heart.

"I'm sorry," he whispered, though he didn't understand the details. Just that the town would be engulfed by the guards, possibly destroyed.

Zehra shrugged. "I'm not afraid to dance in Barzhat's golden court. My life has been short but sweet, and I've tried to do the right thing. But my people..." Her voice trailed off in sadness.

"If I brought them to Hayalevi, would they be safer?" Trulliç asked.

Zehra shook her head. "Most won't leave. This is their town, where their roots are strongest. And many more would stay just to fight."

Trulliç shivered, knowing that the woman spoke the truth. He could feel the wave of support for him, the desert magician, swelling.

"How long do we have?" Trulliç asked. Maybe he could get more men here. Or raise guards. Or maybe walls around the city. Something, anything, to protect his people.

"Three days," Zehra proclaimed, easily pronouncing his doom. "The emperor will wash against your shores in three days."

Trulliç stood stoically still, not letting himself gasp, though her words felt like a solid blow.

Three days? How could he get ready? He didn't even know what he needed to do in order to be ready. He found himself panting, his heart beating rapidly.

Then he paused, making himself take a deep breath, peering curiously at Zehra. *Wash against your shores.* What an odd way to talk about a desert state.

"I will do everything in my power to be ready," Trulliç said solemnly when he realized that she was waiting for him to say something. He couldn't promise more than that. He still didn't know what he was going to do.

"Thank you," Zehra said. "Now, I have a boon to ask of you."

"If it's in my power to grant, it's yours," Trulliç said. He couldn't deny his people anything.

"Give me this hour to enjoy the hospitality of my town," Zehra said. "Nothing more."

"Gladly," Trulliç said, though as they started walking back up the hill leading from the desert to the town, he realized that he'd been lying.

He felt a pressing need to get back to Hayalevi. Raise walls, defenses all the way around the entire border of the desert. Do something, *anything*, other than to sit with strangers and drink tea and eat flatbread slathered in lard.

But he smiled the entire time he was there, chatting easily with everyone, telling of Hayalevi, the secret places of the desert, what it felt like to travel so fast over the land, how he'd originally stopped the emperor's garrison with glass balls that rose out of the sand.

About halfway through the meal, Trulliç realized how focused Zehra was on him. She was very attentive, filling his cup, lightly touching his knees when she leaned closer, how she teased him subtly.

It finally occurred to him that she might want to bed him. He flushed at the thought. She smiled at him and touched his leg again.

If the circumstances had been different, he might have accepted. But Nadeem sat on his other side, a distant presence that still felt as solid as a mountain. Not that he'd made any offer to Nadeem: he was too afraid she'd reject him. And then where would they stand?

Plus, the emperor was coming. Trulliç didn't have a night to spend with Zehra, even in pleasure.

Three days was all he had.

He had to make the most of it.

CHAPTER TWO

NADEEM

NADEEM SAT IN SILENCE, WATCHING Zehra and her party at a distance.

The breach felt impossible to cross. It was only a few feet of sand, but Nadeem knew if she tried, the distance would grow longer and longer with each step.

Zehra wanted so badly to sleep with Trulliç. And maybe that would be the best thing for the boy, to get more of his emotions out of the way, give him some release.

It wasn't as if Nadeem had given him any encouragement, or even hope of a relationship in the future. She couldn't promise him a future. In fact, she was pretty sure that death had just been postponed. She'd be back, ready for Barzhat's embrace, in three days-time.

It didn't make sense to her to fight her way back to life. Not when the emperor was coming. Not when an untrained boy was supposed to be leading the battle. Not when the myth lands still called to her in her dreams every night, clamoring for her soul.

Riyune lay just behind Trulliç, as still as a statue. Trulliç had told Nadeem of his dream the night before. She could easily imagine a carved figure laying in the same position as Riyune did, guarding the steps of the towers of the old kings.

As if hearing her thoughts, Riyune slowly turned a stoic face toward her. Then he deliberately cocked his head to the side, looking for all the world like merely a puzzled dog.

Nadeem laughed once, briefly. The man sitting beside her—Ebrhard? Ecklin? E-something—shot her a quizzical look.

Nadeem just shook her head, keeping her commentary to herself.

Riyune had his own secrets. Just as she had hers. Though the laughter had felt good…

Nadeem shivered and pulled herself back.

No.

She would stay separate. Apart. Until the world ended.

In just three days-time.

<hr>

All the journey back to Hayalevi, Nadeem thought about teasing Trulliç by imitating Zehra. *Oh, Trulliç, how strong you are! How wonderful your magic is!*

But that would mean stepping across the gulf, interacting with Trulliç more than Nadeem felt comfortable with.

They'd told Myrizhah and Seydat about Zehra's dreams of the emperor arriving in three days. The other women grimly nodded.

"Should we prepare for siege?" Myrizhah asked, breaking the deadly quiet that had consumed them all.

"That would mean raising walls all the way around the city," Trulliç said. "Osmerli had a great wall, and it didn't save them. Plus six kings."

"I could go to the Kardeş oasis and ask the star sisters for help," Nadeem offered to Trulliç. "I don't know if any will come. They are dedicated to the emperor. They might try to kill me. But some—some will come with me."

The thinkers would follow her, not the fanatics. Plus, the star sisters were desert creatures, like Nadeem, like Trulliç. Their loyalties would be divided.

Every time Nadeem had made the offer to go recruit the star sisters over the last couple of weeks, Trulliç had declined. He didn't want the star sisters here. They weren't truly his people, at least, not all of them.

Now, as the time for the battles drew near, he finally acquiesced.

"Bring them," he said. "Those who would be loyal to me. Who wouldn't betray me to the emperor."

"The number is likely to be small," Nadeem warned.

Trulliç gave a bitter laugh. "It will be worthy of a song," he told her. "If any remain to sing it."

Nadeem nodded. Trulliç was right. They were always going to be outnumbered. All that remained was that they died in honor.

The gap between them felt a little wider, suddenly.

"I will return soon," Nadeem promised.

"Take Riyune with you," Trulliç said.

"What?" Nadeem asked, startled. How could she? It wasn't as if she could tie a leash around the ghost dog. Or even a collar. And it wasn't as if Riyune would willingly travel with her.

Trulliç had turned and addressed the dog directly. "You need to go with Nadeem. Make sure she gets to Kardeş fast, and returns even more quickly, with whomever will follow her."

Riyune gave a great dog sigh, then cocked his head to one side, as if questioning what Trulliç wanted.

"Protect her," Trulliç added. "Like a blood hound with his charge."

Instead of responding, Riyune stood and stretched like a dog, butt in the air and front paws out, then he stood straight up and shook himself.

He glanced again at Trulliç before walked beside Nadeem, then collapsing beside her with a loud *huff.*

Riyune knew exactly what Trulliç had asked. Nadeem was certain of it. Did he act like such a dog in order to throw the humans off his scent? Or was being a dog his nature as well? Not merely a false disguise he wore?

"Thank you," Nadeem said, first to Riyune than to Trulliç.

She didn't know if she could get anyone other than Aunt Parayat to follow her. But even at her great age, her aunt would be fantastic help.

Even if it meant dying in the process.

yrizhah packed a simple bag for Nadeem with traveler's food, like the log-shaped rolls made out of cracked wheat, hazelnut pieces, and slivers of dried figs, spiced with mint and nutmeg, all held together with *meslit* syrup, as well as salted meat and more nuts.

The flagon Nadeem carried was small for such a journey. Then again, like Trulliç, Nadeem knew she could always find water in the desert.

She kept on the same outfit she'd been wearing earlier, a more traditional whitish-blue blouse under a gold-and-green striped sleeveless tunic, her wide leather belt with the three knives, but matching it with the black leggings of the star sisters so she could run and fight without hindrance. She wore a black-and-white checked *chafiyek* that she'd wound over her nose and mouth so that it would be easier for her to breathe the desert air as she traveled.

Nadeem and Riyune stood next to Xanil's temple, near the eastern gate of the city. It was only a simple archway, not a formal gate for a walled city. During the past two weeks since they'd come back from the myth lands, caravans had started arriving. They entered the city from the east, as it was only a short distance from the border beyond the desert sands. Plus, the path followed the bubbling Pirazizil river, so they would always have water.

The western gate was far less frequented, as the travel to there from the lands outside the desert would take more than a week's time. In addition, while a string of oasis lay along the trail, water wasn't always guaranteed, particularly during the summer months.

"Ready?" Nadeem asked, glancing down at the dog sitting beside her.

He looked up at her, his bright pink tongue lolling to one side.

Nadeem rolled her eyes at him. It was hard to accept that Riyune was both a dog as well as something else sometimes, particularly when he acted so much like an animal.

"Let's go," Nadeem said.

Nadeem raced out of the eastern gate, Riyune at her side. She felt her feet lift higher, her speed increasing.

So it seemed that the dog had the same ability as Trulliç, to grant her speed.

Had he always had this capability? Or had it only developed once the dog had been killed in the myth lands?

Nadeem didn't know or really care. This was a trip for the ages. She wished she could take on her favorite illusion form, that of a great hawk with blue feathers, and fly across the land. She gave a great cawing cry.

The rocks and sand blurred as she speeded along. The wind cut at the wound on her cheek that would never heal. She smelled her own sweat as they curved to the left, cutting up the trail leading to the lands beyond the desert.

Suddenly, Nadeem felt her feet slowing. She tried to push on, but was out of breath, as if she struggled against deep sand.

She came to a stop and glared at Riyune. "What is it?" she asked, wary.

Riyune stood like a white marble rock, his gaze fixed on something ahead.

Nadeem squinted her eyes against the bright sunshine. A caravan was making its way down the trail.

She recognized its leader. Levent, the trader that she'd spent a sweet time with, many lifetimes ago.

Her heart lurched and her stomach dropped. Panic washed through her for a brief moment.

She did *not* want to continue her relationship with him. She didn't really even want to see him. He would try to bring her feelings back to the surface, to make her live again.

Then she laughed at herself. Levent couldn't make her do anything she wanted to do. He'd never had that ability.

Instead, Nadeem raced toward him and the rest of his crew, eager to see him again.

Levent's black hair still curled around his face, giving him a smile younger than his twenty-eight years. His dark eyes were filled with joy looking on Nadeem. His caravan had grown smaller over the time he'd been traveling, probably selling everything he could before making the journey across the desert to Hayalevi, being unsure of water or welcome.

"Greetings, traveler!" Levent called gaily as he easily slid down the side of his great camel. "So good to see you again!" He strode broadly up to Nadeem, his arms held in front of him, his hands open wide.

"Good to see you too," Nadeem said, clasping wrists with him like the soldiers did.

"I told you I was on my way to see the city of the great desert magician," Levent said with a broad wink. "Not that I was merely hoping to run into you as well."

"Trulliç is here," Nadeem said. She hesitated, then added, "He's preparing for war."

Solemnity took over Levent. A hard edge appeared as well, his jaw tightening, his eyes growing harsh. "I know. I've shared the dreams of the desert magician. I'm here to offer my services."

"Thank you," Nadeem said, relief making her knees weak. "Thank you, thank you, thank you."

"You are most welcome. And where are you off to?" Levent said. He glanced at her, then at Riyune. "Surely this isn't the creature you're riding?"

Nadeem couldn't help but laugh at Riyune's outraged expression. "No, but he does help me fly," she said.

Levent gave her a curious look but she didn't have time for more explanations.

"Go see Trulliç. Tell him that Nadeem sent you. That Nadeem…will vouch for you," she said.

"Are you certain you want to make that claim?" Levent asked. He'd returned to his serious mien again.

"I am," Nadeem said. Whatever else Levent might be carrying, he'd always had a good heart.

"Very well," Levent said. He stood up even straighter, as if a soldier presenting himself for inspection, then he bowed his head to her. "For you, I will offer Trulliç all my services. Including being a former captain in the emperor's army."

Nadeem stiffened. She hadn't realized he had a military background. Except, maybe she had known, at some level.

Levent didn't walk. He marched.

"Again, a thousand thanks for your offer," Nadeem said. She pulled one of the smaller obsidian knives from her side. "Trulliç should know you speak the truth, but if he needs convincing, give him this."

Levent took the blade reverently with both hands. "I look forward to returning this to you when next I see you," he said.

Nadeem nodded. She did, but didn't, look forward to their next meeting. While he was a delightful man, charming, intelligent, and inquisitive, he was also a painful reminder of the gap between where Nadeem existed and the life on the other side.

"Riyune!" she called, turning toward the dog.

Riyune gave the equivalent of an eye roll, then stood up from where he'd been sitting at her side. He shook himself, the sand flying from his white fur. Then he snapped his jaws together, as if asking, *Are you finally finished?*

"See you in Hayalevi!" Nadeem called as she started to race away.

She risked a single glance back after just a few moments, when the caravan had already retreated into the far distance. She could just make out Levent staring after her, like she was some sort of mythical creature.

And maybe she was. She still hoped that maybe someday, someone would sing songs about the great works that the desert magician and the former star sister had done.

But for now, she had to go persuade as many of her sisters as she could to join her and Trulliç and stand against the emperor.

Before it was too late.

Nadeem didn't bother stopping at the border of Kardeş, though she knew she should. She flashed by the guards, both those hidden in the foothills as well as the two obviously standing in her path.

She had to admit she admired the ingenuity of the two main guards, as well as their training. They knew that they'd never be able to catch the wind speeding toward them. Instead, they stood stock still, then abruptly pulled a hidden rope between them, meaning to trip her as she passed.

The rope snapped on impact. Both guards fell back, having leaned too much of their weight on the rope.

Nadeem wanted to tell them that it was all right, she wasn't going to harm the sisters, but she didn't have time. Instead, she continued her racing steps, Riyune a white blur beside her, as she approached Aunt Parayat's small tent. She didn't bother slowing until after she was inside.

The world reeled as Nadeem came to a halt. She'd grown too used to everything moving in a blur. Everything seemed darker as well. The evening had already fallen, and there weren't many lamps lit in the tent.

Aunt Parayat sat on her teacher's cushion, her tea beside her. She seemed startled to see Nadeem. "I'd expected death to come racing toward me that way," Aunt Parayat said dryly. "Not you. At least, I presume you are not death."

Nadeem shrugged. She hoped she wasn't bringing death to the star sisters she recruited, though she knew there was a good chance that she was.

Aunt Parayat didn't rise, but she did hold out her hands in greeting. "It's good to see you," she said warmly. "Please, share what little hospitality I have to offer."

"Thank you," Nadeem said. She looked over her shoulder at Riyune. Since dying in the myth lands, he'd stopped eating or drinking. Had expending so much energy, running himself halfway across the desert, while aiding Nadeem's speed, given him an appetite?

The dog gave her a huge yawn, then sat down directly in front of the opening to the tent, obviously content to sit there as the guard.

"That's a strange creature you travel with," Aunt Parayat said, peering intently at Riyune.

Nadeem shook her head. Her aunt didn't know the half of it. "What do you see?" she asked, curious. Aunt Parayat was stronger than most, particularly when it came to seeing through illusions.

"I see—"

One of the guards who Nadeem had raced by suddenly came into the tent.

Riyune stood and barred the way. For the first time ever, Nadeem heard the dog growl. It was the sound of a deadly predator, much larger than its victim. The noise made the hairs on the back of her neck rise up and set her blood racing.

The dog suddenly grew larger as well. Instead of being the size of a regular dog, its back rising level with Nadeem's knee, now Riyune was the size of a fierce lion, his back level with her waist. And Nadeem wasn't short.

Only the blood hounds had the ability to change size that way.

"Put your weapon away, Mojin," Aunt Parayat directed in a harsh, commanding voice.

Mojin? Nadeem looked at the girl with great curiosity. She'd shared her coming of age ceremony with Mojin, chosen the *ağrikat* mussels deliberately so that as a warrior, Mojin would remain balanced.

Had it worked? What was the girl like now?

Mojin looked startled, but she slowly slipped her knife back into her belt. She wore the traditional all-black outfit of the star sisters, tight fitting so that she could move quickly and fight without impediment.

Only then did Riyune settle down, shaking himself once and shrinking back down to his natural size, before laying down and resuming his guard position.

Nadeem noticed that he was still between Mojin and her, that he could still protect the rest of the tent from his position.

"Ma'am," Mojin said. She swallowed hard. "We saw *her* race toward your tent. We got here as quickly as we could."

"You did your duty as well as you were able," Aunt Parayat said. Nadeem could hear the prideful smile in her voice. "You were just faced with something you couldn't have stopped. That no one could have stopped. The desert wind, itself."

Mojin stiffened. "Yes, ma'am," she said. She cast a look at Nadeem, curiosity mingled with fear. "Don't I know you?"

"We were sisters, once," Nadeem admitted. She turned her face so that Mojin could see her mangled cheek.

The heat of Mojin's stare made Nadeem's cheek pulse with pain briefly.

"I see," Mojin said, though it was obvious she didn't understand in the least.

"Guard the entrance to my tent as diligently as your previous post," Aunt Parayat instructed. "See that no one disturb us. Not even another desert wind."

"Yes, ma'am," Mojin said stiffly before turning and marching out the door.

"We don't have much time before the others come and demand answers," Aunt Parayat said. "Mojin is a sweet girl, strong and warm. She will do her duty and turn them away but they will overwhelm her in the end. What do you need?"

Nadeem's heart gave yet another hard beat in her chest, as if trying to remind her that she was still alive. She stifled her response.

Not now. Not yet. Maybe not ever would it be time for her to fully join the living.

But still, she couldn't help but feel a great rush of gratitude toward her former mentor who didn't ask Nadeem what she wanted, but would happily give her whatever she needed.

"Star sisters," Nadeem said bluntly. "As many as you can recruit. To help defend Hayalevi from the emperor."

"That's a tall order," Aunt Parayat said. "Most are fanatically dedicated to the emperor. They've already received recruitment orders to come and fight for him."

"How many will go and fight with the emperor?" Nadeem asked. Even if none of the star sisters came with her, learning that number may help Trulliç in his fight.

"At least a quarter," Aunt Parayat said.

"Of all the *kabils*?" Nadeem asked, horrified. That would mean thousands of star sisters.

"No, just of Kardeş," Aunt Parayat said.

That still meant hundreds of trained fighters on the side of the emperor.

"Why not all the *kabils*?" Nadeem wondered out loud.

Aunt Parayat snorted. "Because he's as arrogant as any man. He thinks he doesn't need them. He barely put any effort into recruiting the women here."

"Really?" Nadeem asked. It actually made sense that the emperor wasn't afraid of Trulliç. He'd been emperor for at least two centuries, and fighting wars for much of that time, while Trulliç was an untrained, untested boy, still.

"He'll pay for his arrogance," Aunt Parayat said darkly.

Arguing voices could be heard just beyond the tent door.

Riyune gave a quiet, warning growl.

"You need to be gone," Aunt Parayat said. "I give you my blessing, but we'd end up spending days arguing with the others if they saw you."

"Meet me on the eastern hill at dawn," Nadeem said. "With all you can persuade."

"I will," Aunt Parayat said. "It won't be many," she warned.

"Every blade will help," Nadeem said, nodding. She'd always known that she wouldn't be able to bring an army of trained fighters with her, though she desperately wished she could.

Aunt Parayat rose gracefully to her feet. "Now, go. I need to deal with these idiots. I will see you at dawn."

Nadeem nodded. "Riyune," she called.

The dog stayed where he was, though he did glance over his shoulder at her, as if asking, *What now?*

"This way," Nadeem said. She picked up an edge of the tent, cleverly hidden by illusion. All who passed thought Aunt Parayat's tent was firmly staked down.

The dog sniffed, then stood and shook himself. He gave Aunt Parayat a doggy grin, showing all his teeth, then moving as fast as a blur, raced out of the tent without looking back.

Nadeem rolled her eyes. "At dawn," she said one last time before she also raced off into the cool night.

⸻

Patience had never been one of Nadeem's virtues. Still, she waited for the dawn with something akin to it. Riyune napped beside her. Evidently he was similar to Trulliç that way, and seemed to be more energized by daylight than by starlight.

Mice quietly rustled in the grass near her feet. Nadeem listened carefully for the cawing of a hawk, or the soft hoot of an owl. Those sorts of noises would be out of place at this time of night. Though they might sound natural, the calls would be made by star sisters approaching her, groups signaling their readiness.

Winds carried the smells of Kardeş to Nadeem: the watch fires, the scent of sweet girl sweat, the water from the oasis. Would Riyune catch the scent of any attackers before they appeared out of the darkness? Nadeem wasn't sure.

Her legs ached due to all that she'd asked of them today. She stretched them while she waited, tightening the muscles then releasing them, flexing her toes then making them into fists. She'd drunk all the water she'd brought, knowing that she could easily make a trip to an unguarded part of the oasis if she needed more.

And maybe she should get more before they left at dawn.

How many would her aunt bring? A dozen, perhaps? Or maybe only a handful? Nadeem had no idea.

That the emperor wasn't taking Trulliç as seriously as he should may be in their favor. Perhaps the emperor would overplay his hand, or extend himself like a beginning fighter, leaving a vulnerable side unguarded.

Nadeem didn't know. She had battled, many times before, in small groups. She'd learned at least some strategy when it came to fighting with larger armies, but she had no actual experience either.

She hoped that Trulliç would at least listen to Levent, particularly when the merchant handed over Nadeem's blade. Surely Trulliç wouldn't be a complete idiot about it, and wouldn't instantly be jealous of Levent and not want to work with the man.

Nadeem counted heartbeats as the stars moved slowly overhead. She even laid down for a bit, flat on her back, so she could see them better. The sand felt cool, welcome against her skin. The pounding in her cheek subsided as if the desert winds were a cool balm. The smell of the nearby *meslit* trees, a sweet spicy smell, washed over her.

Would she be able to rest like this once she was dead? Or would Barzhat cause her to dance forever and ever for breaking a blood oath?

But the oath had been wrong. Nadeem may occasionally have regrets about not fulfilling it, worrying about Trulliç and his anger, however, killing him wouldn't have made anything right.

Would Riyune have stopped her from killing Trulliç? She honestly didn't know.

She'd heard the story of the blood hound who'd created the glass horseshoe that was Trulliç's symbol. Could see it suddenly in her mind's eye, a much younger Myrizhah crying on her birth bed, the hound as large as a small horse beside her, shaking and shaking the tin horseshoe until it changed into glass.

Had there been other babies in the past who'd been promised as the desert magician? Had none of them gotten as far as Trulliç and actually claimed their territory?

Nadeem had the impression there had been. Other babes who hadn't been protected, who'd stayed in one place too long until the emperor came after them. Or the ones who'd been lost the first time they'd stepped into the desert, overwhelmed by the enormity of their land.

Nadeem sat up with a start. Had she been dreaming? What strange questions went chasing through her head, what odd visions.

She suddenly realized her right hand was warm, warmer than it should be. She curled her fingers slightly.

Warm fur slid across her skin.

With horror, Nadeem slowly turned her head.

Riyune now lay against her leg, as she'd seen him do often with Trulliç. Her hand had found his side.

She didn't remove her fingers, but instead, scratched the dog carefully, like other people did with regular dogs.

Riyune gave a contented sigh and stretched out further, pushing himself more firmly against her leg.

Whatever Riyune truly was, his dog nature was part of it, not something forced on him.

Nadeem gave him another skritch before laying back down, content to share warmth, if even for a single night.

***

Nadeem was up before the dawn, waiting nervously on the eastern ridge. Aunt Parayat had to come. Even if it was just herself. Someone would show up. Right?

Riyune seemed grumpy that morning, as if he resenting getting up in the cool, pre-morning air. He didn't growl at her, not exactly, but he did let her know his displeasure by moving particularly slowly.

The eastern sky lightened, with long fingers of pink clouds reaching out. Nadeem kept to her hiding place, making herself wait. She had to be sure that whoever did arrive wasn't part of a trap, so she stayed hidden, out of sight.

When would Aunt Parayat come? Why couldn't Nadeem hear anyone approaching? Surely her aunt would have been able to persuade at least one or two.

Slowly, oh so slowly, the moments passed by. Nadeem kept checking over her shoulder to judge the position of the sun. It felt as though it was climbing backwards, just to thwart her.

Finally, though, the first rays raced across the land.

Nadeem heard the call of a desert hawk, once, twice.

That had been the signal Aunt Parayat had always used when she'd been training Nadeem.

Then a loud, shrieking whistle broke through the morning quiet.

Nadeem started, but resisted surging to her feet and giving her position away. That had been the call of her class, of Mojin and the others, how the aunts would call all the youngsters back to their lessons.

Who had Aunt Parayat brought with her?

Nadeem crept toward the crest of the hill.

Down in the valley, on the opposite side, she saw dozens of star sisters, grouped together, silently waiting. Possibly hundreds stood hiding in the predawn.

Young ones. Old ones. Cooks from the camp. Even those who traveled as merchants for the *kabil*, gathering goods for them.

Nadeem swallowed down the lump in her throat. Her feet itched to run away. She was leading all these fine sisters into death.

But the goddess of death was their friend. She'd welcome them, one and all.

At the front of the line stood Aunt Parayat. She looked as stubborn as a *meslit* tree, but as old as the hills themselves.

Nadeem knew that she'd never see her aunt like this again.

No matter.

At least Aunt Parayat would have the opportunity to die in a battle worthy of the old saga. Of this, Nadeem was certain.

CHAPTER THREE

TRULLIÇ

TRULLIÇ TURNED THE OBSIDIAN BLADE over in his hands once again. He knew it was Nadeem's knife even before the stranger, this Levent, told him. It carried her scent, that promise of quick death and even less sufferance.

"She gave this to you," Trulliç said, repeating himself.

It was obvious that Nadeem trusted Levent. But why? Was it because he was tall and handsome, charming even Myrizhah? Clever too, given the word play he'd exchanged with Seydat. Or was it because of his military bearing? The discipline at the man's core, that he carefully hid with an easy going smile?

Levent was dressed as a merchant, in a loose striped tunic and baggy pants, all in shades of brown, with a *chafiyek* of gold and green. His proud nose stood up from his face and would have given him an arrogant air if not for his charm.

"I appreciate your offer," Trulliç said as he reluctantly handed the knife back to Levent. They sat at the base of Trulliç's tower, the merchant having been greeted and given hospitality by Myrizhah and Seydat before they bothered Trulliç and told him that he had a visitor. "You know the odds we face, yes?"

He wanted to take Levent's offer of help up so badly. But it wouldn't be a fair exchange. What could Trulliç offer Levent in return for his knowledge, and probably, his death?

Myrizhah came back into the room with tea. The calm mint scent flowed over Trulliç as ten thousand questions bubbled inside. Who was Levant? What did he mean to Nadeem? Were they involved?

Trulliç didn't have a claim on the former star sister. Yet his insides twisted at the thought that she'd given herself to this merchant and not to Trulliç, despite the fact that Trulliç hadn't asked her for anything more than her friendship.

Levent smiled at Myrizhah and thanked her for the tea, taking an appreciative sip before replying to Trulliç. "I think I understand the odds. All those who share the dreams of the desert magician do. The emperor is coming with an army of thousands, hardened veterans of foreign wars. We will have scant hundreds to meet him, untrained volunteers."

Trulliç nodded and sipped at his own tea. The sweet taste fought with the bitterness he felt. So much that he had planned for his city, his people! Would all his dreams be chased away by the desert winds in a few days? A storm called up by the emperor himself that Trulliç couldn't battle?

"We have some advantages, however," Levent continued as if he was unaware of Trulliç's thoughts. "For one, we have the desert magician. He can control the sands, the wind, maybe even the weather."

Trulliç bobbed his head from side to side. It was true, he had called up great storms when he'd been most angry.

"For another, we are actually here, in the desert itself. While the emperor has traveled these lands, it's been a great while. He's surely forgotten some of what the desert herself will teach us," Levent said.

Trulliç blinked, surprised. He'd been aware that the emperor coming to his territory would give him an advantage. He just hadn't been sure how to use it.

Plus, he kept going back to that phrase that Zehra had used, about the emperor washing against his shores. What did that mean? It had to be a clue about how to fight him.

"Third, you are inexperienced," Levent said before he paused and took another long sip of his tea.

Trulliç stiffened. It was the truth. He finally asked, "Why do you consider my inexperience a bonus?" when Levent didn't say anything more.

"Because the emperor will underestimate you," Levent said seriously. "He will only bring as many men as he thinks he needs to crush you. He won't expect you to be able to put up any serious defense. He's been unopposed by his own people for so long that he'll just assume victory."

"Have you met the emperor?" Trulliç asked.

Levent hesitated, then nodded. "Aye. Once." His eyes took on a faraway look. "The emperor came to see the troops as we returned from Lydae, after putting down a brief and foolish rebellion. The emperor spoke to us, thanking us for our duty." Levent shook his head. "He stood there in that great cloak of his, speaking of honor and how proud he was of all the slaughter we'd committed."

Trulliç wanted to ask about the cloak. It was made from the afterbirths of all the magicians and star sisters, so they could never directly oppose him.

Instead, Trulliç asked the question that Levent seemed to need to hear. "What happened after the emperor spoke to you?"

Levent seemed to still be in his own head. His voice dropped to a whisper, thin and strained. "The emperor killed all the prisoners we'd taken. With his magic. He strangled them all, stealing their breath and life away." Levent shuddered. "It wasn't a cruel death, their ends came quickly. But I'd promised them a fresh start if they'd just turn away from the rebellion and return to the empire. I broke my word."

"No, the emperor didn't honor your word," Trulliç pointed out, instantly seeing the flaw. Surely Levent understood that he wasn't to blame.

Levent gave Trulliç a sad smile and shook his head. "No. I knew I was lying when I made those promises. The emperor had already warned us to take no prisoners. I knew better. But I couldn't stand to kill all those people myself. I wanted to be able to sleep at night."

"Did it help? That the emperor killed them, and not you?" Trulliç asked, curious.

Levent gave a sharp bark of laughter. "You're a sharp one," he said. "No, no it didn't. Not at first, anyway. It was still my fault. Still my responsibility."

He turned to look at Trulliç, his eyes now focused as a hawk's after spying its prey. "Watching the emperor kill those people, though…how he changed while doing it...I don't think the emperor is fully human anymore," he said, his voice going back to a whisper.

"He lives on the death of others," Trulliç said quietly.

"You know?" Levent said, surprised.

"I guessed," Trulliç said. "When we battled his guard in the myth lands, and prevented them from stealing the desert heart, the main guard, Marius, grew stronger as we killed his companions."

Levent nodded. "There were rumors of that as well, of the primary leaders of an army, the generals and such, being able to channel the emperor's magic. And his madness." He shuddered.

"So how do we stop the emperor? Without killing anyone and feeding him?" Trulliç asked, going back to the question that haunted his days and nights.

"I wish I knew," Levent said. "I can help organize what men and women you have. Help you shore up your defenses. But as for fighting magic...that's got to be your call."

Trulliç nodded. "I accept your help," he said.

He'd had a momentary sprout of hope, that maybe Levent could tell Trulliç the secret he needed in order to win the war.

But no. Trulliç still had to discover that part himself.

And soon.

* * *

The night was over half gone, and Trulliç still couldn't sleep. He worried about Nadeem, and if she'd be able to persuade any of the star sisters to join them. He worried about his mother and how long she'd live even if they survived the war. He worried about his people, what a war would do to them, how it would change them.

He glowered at the emperor's staff that still stood in the corner in its thick coating of glass. He imagined it laughing at him, taunting him to just give up now. The emperor had defeated the six kings. What hope did a singular desert magician have?

That made Trulliç sit up. How *had* the emperor defeated the six kings? Everyone always assumed that since the emperor had won, and there were no songs or stories about the war, that the victory had come with an easy, single battle.

Had it been a protracted struggle? Had the six kings almost been victorious, except for a bad piece of luck or an ill wind?

Trulliç pursued that line of reasoning. The kings could possibly change into dogs. Or maybe they were actually great dogs who could change into men. Had the emperor struck at just the right time, in mid-change? Had they been trapped and unable to fight?

Then what? Why did the blood hounds of the emperor resemble the dogs of the kings of old?

Or maybe…Maybe the emperor hadn't destroyed the kings. Maybe he hadn't been strong enough to do so, despite what the legends said.

Maybe the emperor had been forced to into a different arrangement. Maybe he couldn't kill the kings. Maybe he just made them serve him, in their dog form.

It was a horrifying thought. The emperor had been in power for two centuries. Had the kings been enslaved all that time? Serving their most hated overlord?

Was this the emperor's final chance to kill them? Kill Trulliç and kill the kings at the same time? Get to them through Riyune?

Atça would accuse Trulliç of being fanciful, a word that Trulliç had truly grown to hate. And maybe he was being fanciful, spinning out tales like any marketplace storyteller. But he knew that the blood hounds and the old kings were connected. And Riyune had first appeared as a blood hound in the cavern before he'd changed shape into the white and black dog.

Trulliç found himself pacing across his room. He wasn't about to sleep like this.

He knew his mother would tell him to rest, preserve his strength. He didn't need to go racing out in the desert. She didn't understand how the daylight refreshed him, not sleep.

With a great howl, Trulliç became a whirlwind of rage and flew out of the tower, off his balcony and onto the desert below.

Storm clouds gather over his head. Lightning raced him. The smell of baked sand and sudden death washed out from him. He howled with the wind, blasting stones apart.

Why had Atça betrayed him? Lied to him about everything? Abused him and his magical power?

He knew why. Atça had been born greedy. He'd never have enough power, enough money, enough status. He was always grasping for more, as well as pointing out to everyone around him how much he had.

Damn him. Damn him! DAMN HIM!

Trulliç's anger super-heated the sand around him, causing it to explode outward in shards of glass and stone.

Trulliç found himself on his knees, weeping in the center of the aftermath. The sand spread out in waves all around him, as if it was too ashamed to be near him.

He was too angry to cry properly, to mourn for what could have been, as only a few tears fell from his eyes and splashed onto his hands.

Would his anger be enough to stop the emperor, though?

Somehow, he doubted it.

As dawn came, Trulliç ate a small bit of flatbread while Myrizhah, Seydat, and Levent formed plans. He had very little to offer, except in terms of logistics. Sure, he could move people wherever they needed to go. Water wouldn't be much of an issue, as he could always raise wells. Food was more of a concern, as he learned that an army marched on its stomach. But Seydat and Myrizhah had already started to deal with that.

Could Trulliç cut off the emperor's supply chain? Not when they traveled outside of the desert. Once they crossed the border, though…

Trulliç thought he heard someone call his name. He sat up straighter, brushing away the few crumbs that had landed in his lap. He wore the brown pants again, as they seemed clean enough to him. But to please Myrizhah, he'd put on yet another tunic, this one made from a cloth that had been dyed green, with gold stripes embroidered into it.

Then he thought he heard something again.

Was that Nadeem? Calling his name?

Trulliç ignored Myrizhah telling him that he couldn't just leave as he got up, walked around the guard stone of the tower, and looked out.

There. Nadeem *had* been successful. She had a few hundred star sisters with her. But if Trulliç wanted their help, he had to transport them to the city, and then to where the fighting would be the worst.

"I'll be right back," Trulliç called over his shoulder as he disappeared. He could only imagine the puzzled faces he left behind.

Truly his heart flew as fast as his feet, racing toward Nadeem. She might never return his feelings, but she was worthy of all his attention.

It took him less time than usual to reach where Nadeem and her charges marched down along the western trade route, possibly only an hour. The caravans the star sisters passed all stopped and stared. Few outside of the star sisters themselves had seen so many gathered together in one place.

The star sisters themselves sang fighting songs as they marched. Or they tossed deadly knives back and forth. Some even had drop spindles and spun wool as they walked.

Most wore their habitual black, immodestly tight outfits, though a few of the older aunts wore colorful tunics and *chafiyeks*. Plain leather strips covered their feet, giving them purchase on rough rocks.

The column slowed as Trulliç approached. Nadeem wasn't walking in front, instead, she was about a third of the way back, walking with an elder woman who held herself stiff and proud.

"I am Trulliç," he announced while waiting for Nadeem to come forward. The star sisters at the front of the line nodded stoically at him and stood ready, bearing deadly pikes. Would they attack him if he tried to move among them? They had that look.

The old aunt beside Nadeem sniffed as she drew near, as though she weren't impressed. Still, she told him, "I am called Aunt Parayat. These are my sisters. They are here to fight for you, for the desert, for the goddess Barzhat."

Trulliç suddenly understood why so many of the star sisters had come to serve him. The emperor wanted to become a new god of death. He'd steal away the power of their beloved goddess.

"Thank you," Trulliç said, bowing low. "I am truly honored."

He straightened up, only to find Aunt Parayat looking at him expectantly. "Well? Let's get going!" she instructed him, sounding as imperious as Atça.

"Yes, ma'am," Trulliç said, biting down on his anger. This was someone who meant a lot to Nadeem. He couldn't just blast her for what appeared to be her nature. He needed this old woman, even if she reminded him of his former mentor and tormentor.

Trulliç closed his eyes and reached out with his senses. He found all the star sisters there on the road, felt their cool strength and slippery magic. "Stay steady and strong!" he called out in a booming voice. There was no other warning he could give them before he caused them, as a large group, to all rise above the ground.

Then, just because this Aunt Parayat had demanded that he get going, he sped them all away to his city, going much faster than he had with the soldiers.

Hopefully Nadeem would understand and forgive him.

"That was quite an experience, young man," Aunt Parayat said. Her dark skin didn't hide how her cheeks glowed. Her eyes sparkled with excitement. "How exhilarating!"

Trulliç wasn't sure what to say in return. He'd expected to be scolded, that was what Atça would have done. Not praised, with several of the women looking as though they wanted to do it again, right now.

"I'm glad it suited you," Trulliç said. And he was, mostly. Maybe a tiny part of him was disappointed that the sisters hadn't been scared. Then again, maybe he should have considered what he knew of their training.

A trip through the air was no different than scrambling up and down the cliffs along Knife Ridge. Or even winning their long illusionary battles.

"You may have to take another ride soon," Trulliç finally said as he turned toward the main tower with Aunt Parayat and Nadeem beside him. Riyune trotted after them, looking as satisfied as any dog after a successful hunt.

Aunt Parayat just looked at him with a single arched eyebrow.

Really, she looked more imperious than any of the queens and great heroines he'd read about. And she had been Nadeem's mentor? No wonder Nadeem had such a cool edge to her sometimes.

"The emperor will probably attack from the northwest," Trulliç said. "That's the direction Zahra saw them coming in."

Aunt Parayat shook her head. "That will be the first wave," she said. "He will split his troops as he has in the past. It's easy for him to do a two or three pronged attack, as he can coordinate with his generals using his magic."

Trulliç felt himself rocking back. More than one front? But he barely had enough people and resources to protect the first!

Maybe that was what Zahra had seen. That her town would fall as Trulliç directed his forces elsewhere.

He shook his head. He *hated* this. People were going to die. Innocent people. Good people. *His* people. And there wasn't any way he could save them all.

Aunt Parayat and Myrizhah got along just fine, as Trulliç knew they would. He was more interested in how Nadeem would react to Levent working as Trulliç's primary military commander.

However, nothing but friendship appeared to flow between the pair of them. That, as well as admiration. Levent appeared to greatly respect Nadeem, as he should. He instantly charmed Aunt Parayat as well, the pair of them comparing notes about the wild antics in their pasts.

Nadeem sat at her removed distance, slightly amused, watching them all. Trulliç had hoped that Nadeem might come all the way back and not be so far away after visiting her star sisters, but she seemed as distant as ever.

It made Trulliç wonder if Nadeem would ever come fully back. Or if she'd deliberately sacrifice herself during one of the battles.

What could he do to stop her? There wasn't time!

At least Trulliç felt as though he was making progress on his side of the war. People were being divided up. Fighting orders were issued. The star sisters would split up into three groups, leading his people, the ones who'd volunteered to join the war.

And more people continued to pour into the city. Normally, Trulliç tried to greet everyone who came. But now masses arrived, like a swollen river. He had to leave the war council to go raise more buildings for his people to live in.

One of the star sisters, a young woman named Kalil, asked Trulliç about knives and weapons. She was petite, shorter than most of the other star sisters. Her hair was brown and her eyes were hazel, like his. Was she of mixed birth? Her mother of the desert and her father from Lydae?

"I work with rock and glass," he explained. "Not iron or leather."

She bent her head to the side and regarded him. Then she pulled out her obsidian blade. "This is glass, isn't it?" she asked.

Though Kalil tried to sound innocent, she missed her mark by a long shot. Someone had set her up for this. Had it been Nadeem? Or maybe Aunt Parayat?

But she was right. He could arm his people with glass. Balls they could throw that would explode when they struck anything, as well as obsidian blades.

Why hadn't he thought of it? Instead, he'd been trapped, helpless, as he had been all his life.

"I will make you blades," he told Kalil, trying not to grind his teeth in anger.

It was *not* her fault. He shouldn't be angry with her. Or even at the emperor, really. This had been his problem all along.

"How many blades do you need?" Trulliç asked, trying to modulate his tones. The star sister had taken a step back in the face of his ready rage.

"As many as you can provide," Kalil said. "If they're well balanced, we can use them as throwing weapons."

Trulliç nodded and continued to try to think of the weapons he might be able to form. "It would take too long to form arrows from obsidian arrowheads," he said.

"If you could form shards, we could use them with slingshots, and have a longer range," Kalil said.

"Good, good," Trulliç said. "I'll need to go to the foothills south of here—the Yalçin mountains—to get the materials. Then I'll be back and you can direct me how to shape them."

"Do you need help?" Kalil said.

Trulliç couldn't help but smile at the gleam in her eye. Another of the star sisters who'd truly enjoyed the ride that morning. "No," he said softly. "I would just have to carry you as well as all the materials."

He didn't bother telling her that in the bright mid-afternoon sunlight, he was at his peak for strength. However, he needed some solitary time. He suspected he wouldn't get much time alone over the next few days.

Only two more days before the emperor attacked.

Trulliç shook his head and whirled away, no longer paralyzed by the fear that had held for far too long.

Trulliç looked down from the tops of the foreboding peaks of the Yalçin mountains. The desert spread out to the north in front of him. On a clear day, he might be able to see at least halfway across it, though the heat would cause the ground to shimmer like a mirage.

The air blew cold up here, carrying strange scents of frozen rock and rain. Hawks let themselves be carried for miles on the mixture of winds, their cries thin and feral.

Behind Trulliç, just past the cliffs, the ocean pounded the rocks. He couldn't hear the sound, but he felt it deep in his bones, how the water wanted to tear down the mountains and destroy the desert.

He hadn't meant to come all the way up here. His original plan had been to stop in the foothills. The heights had drawn him, though. He'd learned to always carry a pocket full of sand, something to help power him when he stepped away from the desert.

Crossing out of the desert lands felt different this time, compared to the time he'd gone north, back to Gaadiwala. That time, a light shroud had fallen on his senses, as if he lived in a haze. His thoughts hadn't been as precise. Even the pocket full of sand had only cleared his head somewhat.

Up in these foothill, Trulliç still knew he was no longer in the desert. However, his senses weren't as clouded.

Was that because the area up north was so much closer to the emperor and all the land he'd proclaimed as his? While technically, the desert belonged to the emperor, Trulliç knew the truth: it was his, and his alone.

These mountains felt unclaimed to Trulliç, owned by neither the emperor nor the desert magician. He wasn't about to try to take them, however. It didn't make any sense to expand his lands this way. Particularly when these mountains couldn't provide his people with food.

Obsidian, on the other hand…

To his left stood a tall mountain that had blown its top off. Instead of rising into a peak, it was bowl shaped, with one side rising higher than the other, as if formed by a drunken potter.

Black obsidian rocks lay scattered across the entire valley beside Trulliç. Many had salt-white crystals blooming on the sides. It was the equivalent of a gold mine.

Perhaps the star sisters would like to claim this area, mine it in exchange for providing Trulliç protection.

For now, he couldn't try to make that sort of deal. That was for the future.

Because he was determined there would be a future.

Trulliç hurried down into the valley. He picked up a piece of obsidian, then nearly dropped it when he realized how much heat it had absorbed from the sunshine. After he cooled the rock off with a wind, he picked it up again.

Though it looked like a rock, Trulliç recognized that at its core, obsidian was actually glass. He reached out with his senses and started tugging all the loose obsidian on the plain toward him. He stopped quickly when the pile reached the size of a small hut. He didn't want to be greedy.

He was *not* greedy. Not like Atça.

There was still plenty of obsidian left behind in the valley for others to find and pick up. He had no claim on this land. In fact, he might just tell the star sisters about it, and tell them they should use it, free of charge.

He was *not* greedy like Atça.

Still, Trulliç took a few more moments to run to the far end of the valley, where the land started going up steeply again. The rock formations here were odd. It took Trulliç a moment to figure out what they reminded him of: the rocks that made up the cavern that led to the myth lands had the same appearance, of one rock haphazardly placed on top of the next.

They looked strange, as though some mighty hand had slopped the rocks together. What had caused this? Were they put there by the gods?

Trulliç stopped in front of one that had a manlike shape. Beautiful obsidian decorated the tops and edges.

It seemed more than familiar, though Trulliç was certain he'd never been here before. Had he dreamed about this place?

Trulliç's breath caught in his throat. His heart suddenly started hammering. He found himself panting. The sun beat down on him, making his head swim, instead of bringing him more life.

No. It couldn't be.

Trulliç was aware that it was only his imagination that made the stones in front of him look similar to Atça. But they did. The rock formation had the same tall and proud appearance. White crystals clung to the fringes of the stone that would be the skull, like Atça's white hair. A smooth, broad portion made up the forehead, with a large bulbous nose jutting out. Dark pits, where stones had fallen out, made up the eyes.

Without thinking, Trulliç blasted the rocks with an abrasive desert wind. However, through luck (or maybe by direction of the gods) the wind merely scoured the rocks, smoothing out the part that would be the body, making it appear like the figure had just put on a robe.

Trulliç stood panting with effort. He couldn't keep doing this, reacting with anger over nothing. Atça no longer had any power over his life.

Atça was *dead*. Trulliç had killed him.

But seeing this figure, even if it only had a rough resemblance to the original, had pushed Trulliç back to the place where he was just a small boy, being lied to, fighting every day to maintain himself, his sense of magic and what was true.

Trulliç dropped to his knees. He couldn't fight Atça, or rather, Atça's ghost. It was like fighting the wind. Atça's influence and the memories were constantly there. They would never go away.

How could Trulliç stop feeling like this, though? Stop going back to that little boy who could never do enough to please his mentor? That child who could never do enough, be enough?

How could he free himself?

Tears started streaming down Trulliç's face.

He couldn't have freed himself from Atça's influence. Not before he did.

He *had* been just a small boy. And while Myrizhah couldn't have saved him, Trulliç couldn't have saved himself earlier either.

He'd done the best he could.

Trulliç wailed his grief, his cries echoing off the nearby mountain tops. He'd been a boy. A little boy. And he'd been abused by his mentor. His magic twisted and aborted.

He couldn't have saved that little boy. He could only let the past stay there, behind him, while the man moved forward, protecting the boy forever more.

Trulliç didn't know how long he wept and raged. When his tears finally slowed, he felt as hollow as a glass ball. He swayed with the slightest breeze, exhaustion overwhelming him.

Finally, slowly, Trulliç looked up. The figure didn't resemble Atça as much now. It looked more like an oddly shaped man.

Trulliç pushed himself up to standing. He still felt as though he tilted to one side, unable to be fully upright just yet. Though he felt empty, he also, for the first time, felt more light as well, as though his feet could travel faster, farther. He knew he no longer carried as much of the past with him, sewn to his clothes like Barzhat's golden weights. He'd cried the tears necessary to release them, finally.

Should he leave the figure as it was? Make it look more like Atça? Less so?

In the end, Trulliç decided to leave the figure as it was. He may need to come and talk with this Atça at some point. Or maybe throw rocks at it.

He'd always know that it was here, though. He'd have to make sure that the star sisters didn't touch it, that this pile of rocks was sacred to Trulliç.

Trulliç looked around again. The mountain with the top blown off still rose high above the plane. Obsidian rocks littered the valley. Birds dove down to the softer places below. The smells the air carried were mixed and rich, carrying a wetness from the ocean.

Everything looked the same. That seemed wrong. It should look different.

Except that Trulliç knew that just *he* had changed. He'd been reformed, somehow.

Trulliç found himself straightening up, his back growing tight and rigid.

The emperor be *damned.* While Trulliç had had a lot to fight for before, now, with the chance of a new life, free of some of the influences of his past, he had even more to fight for.

And not just fight, but win.

CHAPTER FOUR

NADEEM

NADEEM DREAMED OF THE OLD kings. She stood on the sidelines as court started for the day. Six proud thrones were arranged in a semicircle at the front of the room, to her right. Each throne was gilded in gold, studded with snowflake obsidian and rubies. Great banners hung on the walls, one behind each chair, with a different embroidered symbol: bouquets of white calla lilies, a tall Ibis, a fierce lion, a great Orca, a distant mountain at sunset, and a series of circles, one inside the next.

Why were there no dogs? Or did the banners represent something different, and not the kings themselves? Maybe the families they came from?

Strain as she might, Nadeem couldn't get a good look at the kings. It was as if fog filled the space where the men might have sat.

She found herself gasping when she turned her focus back toward the crowd. The people here were rich. No one in this crowd had missed a meal recently, as shown by their round, full faces and meaty hands. Their clothing was rich as well, finely spun and embroidered. Many had the coloring of the desert people, dark and familiar, though she recognized a few merchants who'd come from Lydae, blond men and women with faint, blue eyes.

A group of women moved from the sidelines up toward the dais. Nadeem found herself gasping again when she finally recognized this group as star sisters. They moved with the same grace as Nadeem's sisters, their bodies well trained.

They wore black, as her sisters did. But that was where the resemblance ended.

These star sisters were completely covered from head to toe in bulky robes. The *chafiyeks* they wore were also black, and were wrapped around their faces so that just their eyes showed. Each wore a sparkling circlet of silver, with six stars dangling across their foreheads.

Were they marked with a star as well? Or were their cheeks smooth?

Without the star sister mark, they would be able to completely disguise themselves. No man would be safe: he would never know if the woman he hassled could turn around and kill him with the flick of her wrist.

Despite how they were covered, Nadeem found herself envying them. As just their eyes were visible under their bulky robes, they would be well hidden forever.

The star sisters had always been secretive. Maybe, however, they hadn't always lived completely apart from the rest of the world.

Would her sisters rejoin the world if given a chance? She knew that some might leave the sisterhood. They'd get married, have children, and fade into the background, be regarded as completely normal women.

Until need rose and their true nature revealed itself.

Nadeem couldn't imagine such a fate for herself. But for the new ones, just joining, would they have a different coming of age ceremony? Could they live without the mark?

Before Nadeem could ask one of the star sisters here, she found herself plucked out of the dream and placed back in her small room.

With a sigh, Nadeem collected herself. The room remained the same. Her pack sat in the corner, still packed so she could leave at a moment's notice. A small picture of a cat, drawn in charcoal by one of Seydat's children, was still tacked to the wall beside the small glass-covered window. Her sandals lay at the foot of her bed, placed so that she could easily slip them on if she needed to escape quickly.

Though most of the star sisters lived in tents, in temporary structures, Nadeem had still settled here, in a building made of stone. However, everything about the room screamed that it was temporary. Aunt Parayat's tent had more personality, with her small loom in the corner, a basket holding wool that needed to be spun, her teaching matt and even her clothes.

But Nadeem couldn't stay here, could she?

She shivered, recognizing what had woken her so sharply from her dream.

The thought of there being a tomorrow, of something after the war.

There would be no after the war for her, beyond the golden court of Barzhat. She couldn't allow herself to even think of that.

———

Nadeem watched Aunt Parayat subtly take over the war council. She doubted even Levent noticed. But Nadeem knew he approved as his body language changed and he started to defer to her, like a soldier would treat his general.

It was skillfully, masterfully done. Nadeem shared a secret smile with her aunt when she'd just made yet another decision, directing the course of the battle.

Panic struck Nadeem as her aunt looked away. Surely Aunt Parayat didn't expect Nadeem to do something similar? That would be too much like coming forward, into the world of the living.

No, this was wrong. Nadeem didn't panic. She'd rarely even been afraid. What was happening to her?

Nadeem excused herself and left Trulliç's tower. She pushed herself into the shade and leaned against the solid bricks, taking deep breaths. She needed to get ahold of herself. Was she coming too far back? She didn't want to! She sweated through her loose blouse and tunic. The soles of her feet felt sticky in their sandals. Her stomach churned. Was she getting sick? What was wrong?

When Nadeem looked up, she found that Riyune sat quietly at her feet looking up at her. She couldn't read his expression. Was he curious? Worried? Hungry? The council had feasted on roasted chicken for lunch, and he'd turned his nose up at any bones they'd thrown his way.

Nadeem glanced around the immediate area, expecting Trulliç to be standing just a few feet away, his eyes saying more than his lips ever would.

No one paid any attention to her, though. The people of Hayalevi went about their business with an urgent air, everyone preparing to go to war in two days. A merchant with a large cart piled high with blankets bustled off toward the market, while thee workmen went the other way, intent on their discussion of catapults.

Nadeem pushed herself off the wall of the tower and went back inside. But Trulliç wasn't there either.

Strange. Why would Riyune be there without Trulliç? Where was he?

The council all looked up at her arrival. "What news?" Myrizhah asked harshly.

Nadeem blinked. "I don't know what you mean." Why would they expect her to know anything?

Still, that feeling of foreboding and panic washed over Nadeem again.

Something was wrong. Something was very wrong.

Aunt Parayat kept her sharp eyes on Nadeem while she addressed the rest of the group. "We know that the emperor will attack Egreliki in two day's-time, perhaps less. We suspect that will be merely one of the forks of his battle plan. Has he already started his attack elsewhere?"

All the blood rushed out of Nadeem's head, leaving her woozy. Was that what she was feeling? Was that why she panicked? Was the desert in danger? Would she feel that, being a creature from here?

"Where's Trulliç?" Seydat asked quietly.

"I thought…I thought he'd be here," Nadeem said. "I've never seen him separated from Riyune before. Except when Trulliç told Riyune to follow me."

"Does the dog know where Trulliç might be?" Levent asked, curious. He knew there was something special about Riyune, having seen how fast the dog ran beside Nadeem. But Levent hadn't fully accepted how different Riyune was, being the most surprised when the dog had snubbed the bones he'd been thrown.

"If Trulliç was in the desert, he'd know if the emperor had attacked," Nadeem said firmly. "He's left the desert."

"Why would he do something foolish like that?" Myrizhah said, her voice harsh and stern, as though she were addressing the boy Trulliç had been and not the man he was becoming.

"I don't know," Nadeem said. "Maybe the emperor hasn't arrived."

The disbelieving looks from everyone made her feel guilty for speaking such an inane hope out loud.

"I'll go find him," Nadeem said. Surely that was something she could do.

"Please," Aunt Parayat said. "Without the desert magician, all our hope is lost."

Nadeem turned and strode out of the tower. As she expected, Riyune followed her, then sat expectantly looking up at her feet.

"We need to find Trulliç," Nadeem told the dog seriously. "Right now."

Riyune lolled his tongue out the side of his mouth as he considered her.

"Please, help me find Trulliç," Nadeem said, speaking more plainly.

The dog appeared to roll his eyes at her and stood up. He committed himself to a huge yawn, his jaw nearly splitting, before he gave himself a great shake. Finally, he looked back at Nadeem, as if asking, *Are you ready?*

Nadeem rolled her eyes at the dog. "Yes. Let's go."

With a nod, Riyune started running south.

Nadeem followed on fleet feet, hoping they'd get wherever they were going in time.

***

Nadeem had never been in the Yalçin mountains before. They reminded her of Knife Ridge. The stones here were just as jagged. Wild *meslit* bushes grew as tall as trees, with thorns that would cover her entire palm. Birds flew high across the plain, riding the winds. The foothills had more rain than the desert, so there were more bushes. However, hot desert storms still scrubbed the more delicate plants from the face of the hills.

It would be a good place to train, as Nadeem had out on Knife Ridge, with her old cohort. However, none of her team had come to fight with her. Not that she'd expected they would. They'd all have been recruited by the emperor and would fight for him, instead.

Up Nadeem went, chasing after Riyune, further away from the desert. She found her breath catching as they climbed. Riyune didn't slow down, but Nadeem felt herself tiring.

Was she that much of a desert creature that she could only thrive there? She knew that since she'd rubbed the enchanted sand of the desert into her mangled cheek that her magic had changed. Did she only draw her power from there now? Instead of being a star sister and able to travel and cast illusions throughout the entire Tanesh empire? Was she now bound like a male magician?

No, she should be able to cast her illusions here. It was just her other abilities, her fleet speed and how quickly she could find water, that would lessen away from the desert.

Should she carry a bit of sand with her everywhere she went, as Trulliç had advised her to do? Possibly.

She shook her head.

Only if she survived the coming battles. Only if she chose to.

Riyune climbed a winding trail, disappearing around the next bend ahead of her.

Worried, Nadeem pushed herself to close the distance between them faster.

The hill flattened out into a great empty valley. Trulliç stood about midway across, a huge collection of stones beside him. Riyune sat at his feet, looking back at her. Even from this distance, Nadeem could see the dog's impatience.

Trulliç hurried across the valley to Nadeem, his hands out. "What happened? Are you all right?"

Nadeem stepped forward automatically, taking his hands and clasping them like soldiers and old companions would. "I'm fine," she assured him. "But there's something wrong."

She quickly explained Aunt Parayat's fears that the emperor was attacking using a pronged attack, and that the war had already started.

Trulliç shook his head. "No, even here I would have felt him moving across my land."

"Are you sure?" Nadeem said. "What if his troops were protected, or carrying implements like the emperor's cane?"

Trulliç's expression grew stormy. "We will stop him," he said simply.

Strange. The rage that normally blew off Trulliç didn't follow his statement. He was angry, yes, but stubbornly so. Not like a storm. More like a well-protected city.

Nadeem suddenly became aware that she was still holding onto Trulliç's hands. They felt stone hard and warm in hers, the skin roughened by the desert sand. "What happened to you?" Nadeem asked. She tried to let go of Trulliç's wrists, but he held on.

He gave her a bitter laugh. "I threw myself at the rocks," he said. "Crashed myself to bits so I could be reborn."

Nadeem blinked. Of course. How like a poet, which really was Trulliç's soul. "I'm glad," Nadeem said. She tugged lightly at Trulliç's hand, willing for him to let her go before she made him.

"But what about you?" Trulliç asked, still sounding maddeningly calm. "How will you come back?"

With a quick twist of her wrists, Nadeem freed herself. It seemed that Trulliç hadn't been holding on that strongly.

"No," she found herself saying. She wrapped her arms around herself, hugging herself tightly. "No," she said again. She couldn't come back, just to let go again.

"There won't be much to continue with, if you're gone," Trulliç said quietly.

Nadeem found herself shivering, as if cold winds had sprung up and were caressing her.

"I need you in my life," Trulliç continued. "I want you by my side. Now and always."

Nadeem shook her head. "You don't want me," she said, her voice sounding as harsh as the sand scoured rocks. "You want some idea of me."

Trulliç laughed, the sound lighter and freer than she remembered. "I don't believe that's true," he said. "But even if it is, I still love the you that you'll become after the war."

Nadeem shivered again mightily. After the war. That was the problem, wasn't it? There was no after the war for her.

Aunt Parayat would accuse Nadeem of a failure of imagination. She couldn't see an after the war for any of them.

"Come back to me," Trulliç said softly. "Come back to the world. There is much goodness here, much to love. Even if you don't, can't, love me. Even if you want to stay out on your own, or find your solace with someone else. Return to me. Please."

No one had ever asked Nadeem to be with them. Her old team, the star sisters she'd trusted with her life, had turned their backs on her, betrayed her, would kill her given the chance.

"I can't," Nadeem said, her voice cracking. She couldn't trust this, couldn't trust Trulliç. "At least, not yet."

"Thank you," Trulliç said, his voice warm and filled with contentment. "You've at least given me hope with that 'yet'."

Nadeem shook her head and finally turned away from the rock wall to face Trulliç again.

She could see the changes now, how tall he carried himself now, his back unstooped and his shoulders relaxed. His face had fewer worries, even with the coming war.

"We need to get back to Hayalevi," Trulliç said.

"Why did you come here?" Nadeem asked. "Surely it wasn't just to break yourself into a million pieces."

Trulliç laughed again, the joyous sound carrying around the bowl of the valley.

Nadeem suspected that she could get used to the sound of that laughter.

"I came up here to gather obsidian for the star sisters," Trulliç said, indicating the pile of stones she'd first found him beside. "This land is unclaimed," he added, indicating the entire ridge. "It doesn't belong to the desert. It really doesn't belong to the emperor, either. I don't know if you can feel the difference, but I can."

Nadeem thought for a moment. Yes, the mountain she stood on wasn't part of the desert. She knew that because she wasn't as strong here. But it felt cleaner than the other parts of the empire she'd visited. Was that just the fresh winds blowing off the ocean? Or was it something different?

"I want the star sisters to own in," Trulliç said seriously. "I know, I know, it isn't much to look at. You can't really survive up here."

Nadeem snorted. How little he knew of the resourcefulness of the star sisters. There were plenty of small creatures they could eat hidden in the rocks, rain catchers they could create for the morning dew, how the branches and leaves of some of the nearby scrub would sustain a body.

Trulliç gave her a puzzled look, but went on. "However, you could mine the obsidian up here. Possibly use it for trade."

Nadeem nodded slowly. He was right. She looked out over the valley. Did all those rocks contain obsidian? If they did, that represented a fortune for the sisters, right there. Plus, they could conduct rigorous trials here, in addition to the Knife Ridge training area.

"Why would you give this to us?" Nadeem asked.

"I'm not," Trulliç said adamantly. "It isn't mine to give. It is no one's land. However, I wouldn't object if the star sisters claimed it for their own."

Nadeem appreciated the distinction. Plus, if the star sisters took over these foothills, it would give Trulliç peace of mind, as he wouldn't have to defend this border.

Then again, there wasn't much to attack here. The only access to these mountains came from ships crossing the endless ocean. They'd have to find a port, then scale foreboding cliffs. Anyone who made such a journey would be an opponent worthy of the star sisters.

"I'll let the main council know," Nadeem said. "They will have to decide for all the *kabils*."

Though she couldn't imagine them turning the proposition down, not with all that obsidian just laying around, free for the taking.

"And the other?" Trulliç asked.

What other? Nadeem looked at him curiously.

"You'll let me know if you decide to be my companion? My love? My wife?" Trulliç said, his voice quiet but firm.

"I will," Nadeem said, feeling herself still shaking inside, though her body remained steady, not betraying the strong emotions clashing through her.

What had Trulliç said about breaking himself into a million pieces against the rocks up here?

Nadeem hadn't broken completely apart. But she'd started the process. A crack had formed in her protective shell, that distance she'd been holding everyone at since nearly dying in the myth lands.

And though she could patch that hole back up, for the first time, she wasn't sure she wanted to.

***

Nadeem enjoyed racing down the mountain with Trulliç, more than she should have. But it was fun to glide so fast between the rocks, to tease Trulliç by racing ahead, then letting him catch up. The winds blew easy against her face. Though her cheek ached, it was a good pain, like the kind her muscles had when she'd been training long and hard.

Everything changed, though, once they reached the desert proper. Trulliç's face grew serious. Nadeem saw the man behind the boy, how he would mature over the years. He didn't have as handsome a face as Levent's. Trulliç had the tall, proud nose of the people of the desert, their darker skin, eyes and hair as well. His thin lips could be very stern, or very playful.

It was an intelligent face. His body was long and hard after living in the desert, all the water squeezed out of it. But underneath it all, he still had the soul of a poet.

Could Nadeem live with a desert poet the rest of her life? That would possibly be easier than with a desert magician. Maybe someone would write songs about the mighty deeds they did together.

Nadeem could be content with that.

Still, Trulliç hurried toward Hayalevi, his great pile of stones flying with him. He went first to Barzhat's temple, where the star sisters had camped.

As soon as he touched down, several of the guard ran forward. "Take these," he said. "Shape them quickly. I'll be back to help if I can."

Then he turned to Nadeem. "I can't tell for certain," he said slowly. "But the emperor, or at least some of his guards, may be here. They're well-disguised. But something is wrong."

"I'll go inform the council," she said, turning.

"Good. Gather a third of the defenders and bring them here in an hours' time," Trulliç said.

"Where are you going?" Nadeem asked. Trulliç appeared to be walking right beside her, hurrying back toward the magician's tower.

"I need to go master a cane," Trulliç said with a grimace. "Or destroy it."

"Good luck," Nadeem said, and she meant it.

Trulliç appeared to transform into a dust devil as he raced away, a spinning collection of sand and wind.

The old Trulliç wouldn't have been able to do anything with the emperor's cane.

This one, however, might have the patience and deep roots within himself to withstand the emperor's slippery magic.

CHAPTER FIVE

TRULLIÇ

TRULLIÇ DID NOT GIVE HIMSELF time to think. He raced up the stairs of the tower and into his room, gathering up the glass-encased staff and throwing himself the rest of the way up to the top of the tower.

Sunlight beat down on Trulliç's head, warming his soul. He planted his feet wide, feeling as though roots shot down from the base of his heels, through the soul of the tower, and into the desert below. The stones connected him and his strength. He smelled the baking fires and felt a memory of hunger, how his mouth had once watered for his mother's fine flatbread fresh from the stove.

But that was no longer him.

He studied the case, looking at the cane with great curiosity. He knew it was dangerous. When he broke the glass, the cane would regain its power.

Could it call its master to it? Or even worse, channel its masters power, so that the emperor could blast dangerous magic through it?

Possibly. That was why Trulliç had encased the cane in glass in the first place, so that the errant magic couldn't slip through.

He also realized that he'd merely neutralized the cane. He hadn't stopped it, not really. Like everything else in his life, it had been waiting for him to do something more.

The emperor was coming. Trulliç had to be able to stop him, stop his magic.

The cane would be a good test.

A movement caught Trulliç's eye.

Huh. Riyune had joined him. Why had the dog stayed behind earlier that morning, when Trulliç went up into the Yalçin mountains? Had it been to protect Nadeem? Or had the dog realized that Nadeem was going to have to fetch him?

Trulliç truly didn't know. But Riyune being here made him uneasy. Trulliç wasn't sure why.

He glanced between the glass case floating in the air above the tower, and the dog beside him.

They cast the same sort of wavy shadow. Neither of them were solid things with solid lines.

What magic would fill Riyune when it came time? Was he, too, a vessel for channeling something powerful from beyond?

Trulliç smiled softly at himself when he heard Atça's voice accusing him of being too fanciful. He knew at other times that he'd get angry at the reminder, but for now, it just made him shake his head and push his former mentor away.

He could deal with Atça ghost later. Again.

For now, Trulliç had to focus on releasing the cane, then blocking its magic. Hopefully Riyune wouldn't get in the way.

Trulliç expanded his senses, wrapping them more firmly around the glass case floating in the air. The glass itself was heavy and thick. It had a sheen in the sunlight that reminded Trulliç of the fountain in the courtyard, the splashing water casting the same shimmer.

Inside the case, Trulliç couldn't feel the cane at all. He could see it with his eyes, he knew it was there, in front of him. But he couldn't find it. The cane felt…slippery. As though it wasn't really there, but somewhere in between the world and its place of origin.

Maybe Trulliç could just blast the cane back to where it came from. But that didn't feel right. The emperor could just call it forth again.

No, Trulliç had to *block* the cane from getting through.

But how?

Trulliç called up all his defenses. To the right of him, a wind storm swirled in on itself, ready to lash out and carry the cane far past the desert, even beyond the Yalçin mountains and to the ocean. Another storm, full of crackling lighting, hunched together on Trulliç's left, the power strong enough to damage the tower itself if Trulliç wasn't careful.

He'd even borrowed the largest caldron he could from Seydat, carrying it up to the top of the tower and filling it with water, willing to drown the cane if he needed to.

Beneath where the cane floated, Trulliç had already heaped a small hill of sand, hoping that would at least help him capture the damned thing.

His preparations finished, Trulliç sent a brief prayer to Serril, the god who'd brought all magic to mankind, both the men and the women. He was a trickster god and difficult to appease. But Trulliç felt as though Serril approved of him as the desert magician, as well as the people of his city, those he'd brought into the desolate places. Maybe the god would help Trulliç fight the emperor as well.

Of course, the goddess that Trulliç really needed to invoke was Barzhat, as she stood the most to lose if the emperor won. But Trulliç had never worshipped her and it felt false to suddenly start now.

Trulliç untied the glass horseshoe he always carried with him. It had helped him in the past with his greatest magic. It really didn't have that much magic in and of itself, but it helped him focus.

For now, Trulliç narrowed his attention on the glass surrounding the cane. He knew glass, knew its flaws and its strengths, the heat it needed to make it flow like the sweet *meslit* syrup, the length of time it needed to cool so it wouldn't crack.

The glass melted around the cane, reforming into sand and rock below where the cane floated. Heat radiated out from the sand, making it too hot for even Trulliç to touch, but he took a step forward anyway. The warmth seared his face. He was forced to deflect it before it actually burned him.

However, that extreme temperature didn't melt the wood or the silver of the cane. Whatever it was made from, it wasn't normal. Or perhaps stronger magic protect it.

Trulliç called up a soft, chilling wind. The sand crackled as it cooled, sounding like glass breaking.

Finally the temperature lowered enough that the cane appeared to awaken. Magic slid from the thing. Trulliç knew the cane still floated in the air in front of him because he could see it. That was the only sense that told him where the cane existed. Though it did exude a slipperiness, as though it was made from oil. Maybe he could hone in on that feeling when he tried to detect those with such magic.

Trulliç turned his attention to the top of the cane, the silver head of the snake. Each scale of the small figure looked like the emperor's leaf symbol. What was that snake made out of? It stayed still, but it still seemed to waver in the heat.

Then Trulliç focused on the body of the cane. The wood just below the head of the snake seemed almost normal. If he turned his magical sense to just the wood, he could almost feel it, as if it were closer to him than the snakehead.

A silver cap tipped the bottom of the cane. Like the top, Trulliç found he couldn't sense it with his magic.

Were those two parts of the cane actually connected to some other place? Like how the cavern connected this world to the myth lands, did the cane connect this world to someplace else?

But where?

Trulliç wrapped his sand around the head of the cane. It slid off, as though trying to pile around a steep hill. He tried winds next, but the winds just blew past the cane as if it wasn't there.

And still the cane exuded a power that made Trulliç's skin crawl.

Trulliç caused the cane to turn upside down, then thrust the head into the water. The cane didn't notice it at all. If Trulliç felt like being fanciful, he'd say that the cane laughed at him.

Trulliç brought the cane out of the water and thrust the top of it into the sand.

Ah. There. He could finally *feel* something. Grains of sand rubbed against the wood of the cane, scraping at the black dye. The silver tip was hidden far below. Trulliç couldn't feel it, not exactly, but he could feel *something*.

Why did the sand appear to drown the cane, while the water didn't?

He remembered Zahra's odd phrasing again, about the emperor crashing against his shores.

Trulliç knew he didn't have much more time. The first wave of his volunteer army were about to go out and greet the wrongness that he felt, close to the Kinarak mountains, near Gaadiwala.

Of course, the emperor would strike there first. He should have thought of that. The emperor didn't merely slaughter the men and women of the places he conquered, he also destroyed their dreams.

Did he think that by hurting the people of Gaadiwala that he would hurt Trulliç? Did he not understand that they weren't his people? After he'd killed Atça, he'd given them the choice to come with him to the desert. Only a couple dozen had made that decision, most of whom were part of Trulliç's immediate family, his aunts, uncles, and cousins. The rest had stayed in Gaadiwala.

Killing the people who'd remained in the village Trulliç had been raised in would make him angry, yes, but no more angry than any of the other deaths of the innocents.

No, when the emperor reached Egreliki and killed the people there, that would hurt much more.

Trulliç drown the cane in sand. Something in the sand, like the glass, neutralized its power. Not completely, it still maintained its oily nature. But its call felt distorted, as though the sand tainted it.

He didn't trust the sand to hold the cane, however, so he locked it back up in glass. Thicker, this time, clear and wavy. Then he caused the case to go shooting across the sky into the true desert, then down, into the ground, burying it deeply in the sand, away from any water or true rock.

He would have to fetch it back up later. For now, it was safe enough. He wouldn't have to deal with a foe at his back while the emperor's forces attacked him from the front.

Riyune hadn't done much of anything while Trulliç had experimented with the cane. It was almost as if the dog had merely come to be a spectator, without any commentary.

Did the old kings not know how to deal with the emperor either? Had they been hoping that Trulliç's magic would be enough?

Or had Riyune been here to kill Trulliç if the emperor had taken him over? If his dreams of the old kings had been true and not just his imagination, Trulliç hadn't been the first desert magician they'd tried to help.

And he wouldn't be the last.

Riyune accompanied Trulliç to the temple of Barzhat, where the star sisters and their charges had gathered. Very few of the men looked like hardened warriors, though several of them did have an edge that told Trulliç they were truly people of the desert. Some of the women who weren't star sisters had that same roughness.

The desert wasn't kind or forgiving. Too often, a single mistake would lead to death. The nights of the desert could freeze, while the sunlight blasted and burned.

The people of the desert reflected that, their eyes like hawks studying the horizon for storms or bandits, their noses keenly tuned to any trouble.

They were *his* people. The stillness each held was reflected in Trulliç's own soul. He recognized the depths of their feelings and their cares.

The star sisters were a different breed. The promise of death bound them together, their training and excellence shining through. They weren't as still as the desert people, and much of their roughness had been smoothed away.

Yet, they were here, fighting for him, as well as for their goddess.

Myrizhah stood there with the group. She didn't mean to go with them, did she? But no, she was just seeing to some last minute provisions.

"Thank you," Trulliç said to his mother, stepping up to her.

"For what?" she asked, looking harried, as if she'd planned on hurrying away and now something was stopping her.

"For doing everything that you could for me," Trulliç said. He took her hand and squeezed it.

Myrizhah blinked for a moment, surprised. Then she shrugged. "It needed doing," she said simply.

"Aye," he said, letting go of her hand. "Still. Thank you."

Myrizhah looked at him, puzzled. She seemed to realize suddenly that he was different than before. She gave him a small smile. "Your soft heart may survive yet," she said. Then she was off, back to the tower and the war council, back to keep the home fires burning.

Trulliç found himself the natural center of things as the crowd circled around him. "I don't know what we'll find out there, at the edge of the desert," he said. "I suspect it's part of the emperor's troops. They'll be walking in plain sight, using magic that lets them hide from the desert."

That brought an angry grumble from everyone. The desert shouldn't be trifled with that way.

"There will be hundreds of them. Maybe thousands. Trained warriors, with swords, arrows, pikes and shields," Trulliç explained. "I don't know if we'll be able to stop them, or just to slow them down. But," he continued, his voice turning hard, "they are not my people. They don't belong here. They are not part of the desert. If that means we must kill them all, then we must."

An angry growl from the entire crowd erupted around him.

Trulliç would rather not kill the soldiers coming with this wave. He knew that their deaths would only strengthen the emperor.

However, his people needed a victory as well, just to show them that it was possible. His war council had decided that the other parts of the army would get different instructions.

This group, the ones led initially by the desert magician himself, would cause the most causalities. They would have receive the most as well, being the tip of the spear.

All of the people surrounding Trulliç carried some symbol of his, whether a glass marble buried deep in a pocket, a small amulet made of glass, or even a glass shard, sharpened and ready to be used like a knife. The star sisters all had pieces of obsidian with them, making them easy to find.

"Then let us war on those who would invade us!" Trulliç called, using a booming voice, aided by the desert winds.

The cry that rose up deafened him.

With the sun still beating down on his head, Trulliç effortless lifted his people up as one.

And flung them toward battle.

As Trulliç had suspected, the emperor's soldiers weren't trying to walk stealthily. It was easy to spot them from more than a mile away, high in the sky. Why they walked across the desert in the bright sunlight, he didn't know. Maybe it was because they were unlikely to meet other travelers at this time, or maybe they were just that arrogant, thinking the sun wouldn't beat them.

However, Trulliç and his group were able to hide. The star sisters kept them disguised, the guards never looking up.

Trulliç gulped dryly when he saw the lines of the soldiers stretching on and on.

He hadn't been exaggerating when he'd said there would be thousands of the emperor's men for every hundred of his own.

The group traveling with Trulliç stayed eerily silent, as quiet as the desert night. Trulliç didn't know that such a large group of people could be so noiseless. Then he realized it was because they were reflecting his own mood, the fierce rage that held him still.

Trulliç set them all down in a valley. The soldiers would come this way, marching in a ridiculously direct line. None of the trade routes were that straight, then again, they followed the course of whatever river ran deep beneath them.

It didn't take long for Trulliç to hide the first third of his people under the sand. They had reeds they could use to breathe were used to staying still. They would start the ambush.

He wished he had more time to pray for them and their souls. They were likely to carry the brunt of the attack. He suspected most of them wouldn't survive.

Then he whisked the star sisters away, placing them past the end of the line of soldiers. It would be likely to confuse the soldiers and to make them think that a much larger army attacked them if they were forced to fight at both ends of their line.

It frightened Trulliç when he realized just how many men they were facing. Well over two thousand. He needed to stop this breach. These men carried large amounts of magic. They had that same slippery feeling that he'd felt from Marius and his squad. He wasn't sure what they could do. Would they channel the emperor? Draw on strength that was not theirs? Once they started dying, would the survivors grow stronger?

That was part of the reason why Trulliç led this attack. He needed to learn as much as he could about the emperor and his forces, as quickly as he could. And while he wanted to bury all the soldiers in sand and not let them attack, his war council had advised him to let the battle play out. He would lose people, yes, but he'd gain information in exchange.

It wasn't a fair exchange. After much arguing, Trulliç had agreed to it.

He'd also insisted on being there, at the start. So he could bear witness to the sacrifices his people made. Aunt Parayat had agreed and had insisted on it as well. Trulliç needed to be there to give his people hope, so that they'd fight for him.

The star sisters were trained to fight and die. His people had never had to fight anything greater than a winter storm or maybe drought, mighty forces on their own, yet not the same as battle veterans.

Trulliç cast the last third of his people along both sides of the emperor's army. They'd commit more scattered attacks, dashing in out of nowhere, taking out a single soldier, then whirling away again. The soldiers wouldn't know what hit them, and wouldn't know where the next attack would be coming from.

Riyune stayed with this group, something that surprised Trulliç. He'd expected the dog to stick by his side.

But as soon as Riyune touched the desert sand, he grew in size, his spine easily reaching Trulliç's waist. He seemed to shimmer in the bright sunlight, an unearthly glow. He growled deep in his chest, a menacing warning that sent shivers down Trulliç's back.

Something that Levent had said stuck with Trulliç. *Fear is in the mind of the enemy's commander.*

And Trulliç intended to push those seeds of fear deep into his attackers.

T rulliç felt the first death as if it were his own.

He'd stayed up and away from the start of the battle. He floated above the attack, getting a bird's eye view of the battle. He'd wanted to be closer to the ground, but he'd acquiesced at the insistence of Beyzha, one of the star sister "aunts" who'd stayed with him. She'd battled beside the emperor's soldiers at one point in her long life and could give him advice about their tactics. It was important that he protect her, because her insights after the battle would be as useful as his own.

She didn't seem that old to Trulliç: her dark skin didn't hold many wrinkles, and her body was as muscular as a man's. Her eyes, however, gave away her age, holding secrets and pain in their dark depths. She dressed in all black, a tight outfit that allowed her movement. In addition to her knives she carried a bow, with arrows tipped with obsidian heads.

It had been exciting to see his people suddenly rise up out of the sand. They slayed the soldiers nearest them without too much commotion.

Then the soldiers started to cry out orders. The enemy was in their camp, beside them, surrounding them.

They quickly changed formation: instead of being a long line, they clumped together, shields out and locked in place.

Trulliç saw his opportunity and took it, before Beyzha could say anything or warn him against it. He sent a rolling ball of wind down, knocking the soldiers aside like a child's game.

The opening he'd created was quickly filled with his warriors, surging like a spear into the gap.

They died just as quickly, their blood mingling with that of their foes.

The soldiers tried to band together again, but Trulliç continued to harry them with his winds, knocking them aside whenever more than four had gathered together.

His people weren't winning, though there were too many bodies, too much blood, too much confusion for him to say for certain.

However, the soldiers were halted, at least for now, and that was what counted.

Beyzha pointed Trulliç's attention to the north, further back along the line. He flew them that way.

As they traveled, one of the men pointed skyward, towards them.

Beyzha shouted, "I have us hidden! They must be tracking us through magic." She sounded angry that they'd seen through her illusion.

Trulliç nodded. He'd expected many of the soldiers to have magic, possibly even be fueled by the emperor. He darted to the far side and looked back.

A group of eight soldiers had broken off the main group and were loping after them.

"You keep going," Beyzha said. "Drop me off here. I'll take care of them."

"No," Trulliç said stubbornly. "Your report is needed by the war council."

"Then you better drop those soldiers before they reach you," she warned.

Trulliç nodded. He'd been thinking about Zahra's comment for a while now.

He reached out and felt for the sand just in front of the running soldiers. It softened with touch, growing deep and fine. Too soft to hold any weight on top of it.

The first soldier started to struggle as soon as he set foot in the patch. The second and third followed along, not realizing the trap they'd fallen into.

The others, however, easily ran around the area that Trulliç had created.

"Do that again!" Beyzha said, obviously impressed.

A muffled booming sound occurred, followed quickly by two more. Sand erupted from where the three men had been buried.

The sand was streaked with blood, as well as the slippery magic of the emperor. Trulliç hurriedly gathered it all together and sent it flying across the desert, across the border, so it couldn't taint the land here.

He shared a glance with Beyzha. He shouldn't try to bury these men. Maybe others, who had less magic. But not these.

Beyzha fired her arrows at them and took out two more, but ran out of arrows before she could drop the others.

Should Trulliç kill the soldiers who kept coming outright? Except that these were the emperor's special men. Either they would draw power from each other's deaths, or their deaths would fuel the emperor.

Trulliç blasted the oncoming soldiers with bouts of harsh winds, bowling them over and sending them back into the rest of the melee. He would trust that Beyzha would watch for him, warn him if they were coming near again.

In the meanwhile, Trulliç concentrated on how the side battles were going.

Not so well.

The soldiers had dug in quickly, hiding behind pikes and shields. It was impossible for his people to get to them. The soldiers were too well organized.

How were they able to form up so quickly? Or was that part of the emperor's magic as well?

Trulliç didn't send winds to disrupt the men. Instead, he gathered together a ball of sheer energy. It was similar to lightning, but it only contained magic.

What would happen when he dropped that on the soldiers?

The disruption was obvious. Though he'd struck toward the middle of the group, the ends shuddered as if they'd been hit too.

Trulliç followed up with another blast. It appeared to travel through the men, the energy leaping from one to the next where they had locked their shields together.

It was equally obvious this wasn't part of their usual playbook. They weren't used to being attacked this way. They didn't seem to have any idea how to fight something that attacked them as a whole.

The soldiers were used to fighting, however. They broke apart quickly, each man at the ready to defend himself.

Trulliç's people, and some of the star sisters, joined the fight now.

But for every man they took down, the soldiers took down three of Trulliç's. His people just weren't trained that way. The slaughter sickened him. The smell of gore would follow him into his nightmares. Not the cries of the soldiers, however. His people remained quiet, almost silent, as they killed or died. Only the soldiers cried out.

He could drown all the soldiers in sand. Use winds to carry them far, far from his lands. He could distinguish them from his own people.

But then what? They'd just come back. Stronger, sneakier than before.

He had to stop all of them from coming. Before he lost more good men and women.

Trulliç did a quick pass over the end of the line of soldiers. Unsurprisingly, the star sisters had been very effective. While a few stragglers remained behind, most of the bodies strewn across the sands weren't wearing black.

It didn't take much to bury the corpses and blow the sands clean of their blood. The bodies of the star sisters he kept to one side. He wasn't sure what the women would do with their dead, but he wanted to give them the option of gathering them up for their own services.

As Trulliç dropped the last of the soldiers into the sand, he realized that their corpses weren't as heavy as the sisters' bodies. He explained his experience to Bayzha, who agreed that he could step down, out of the air, to go and examine one more closely.

Trulliç felt more at peace with his feet on the ground. While he was still connected to the desert when he flew above it, it wasn't the same as walking across the sands himself.

He hurried over to the closest body. Bayzha stood guard, her eyes constantly scanning the horizon for any threats.

Trulliç turned the body over with a wind, not wanting to touch it himself. Then he gasped.

The man's eyes looked as though they'd been burned out of their sockets. His face was gaunt as well. Even his hands appeared skeletal.

The next body Trulliç reached for appeared more normal. Then, his face started to cave in on itself. Whatever soul or life or essence that had remained with the body was being sucked away.

Damn it! The emperor was still reaching into Trulliç's lands. How could he disrupt this flow?

It was proof tnat the emperor was growing strong even as his men died, as Trulliç had suspected would happen.

He threw up glass around the body. That seemed to break whatever connection the soldier had to his master.

Should he encase the entire area in glass? Would that stop the emperor in his tracks?

But no, when he turned back to the soldier. While encasing the corpse had slowed the progress of the magic, it didn't cut it off completely.

What could he do? What would stop the emperor?

Trulliç shattered the glass around the body, as the man was already dead. Then he ignored the horrible putrefying stench the corpse was starting to give off and focused instead on the armor of the soldier.

Like Magnus, the soldier wore a leather chest plate, dyed red, with a great golden snake's scale in the center of it. He also wore a short leather apron that hung down to his knees, over a shorter, lighter weight, cropped set of pants.

Magnus had been able to remove the snake's scale from the center of his chest. The emperor had focused his magic through it. Could it also be used to suck the remains of a man's life from him?

Trulliç raced down the line, looking for an uncorrupted body. When he finally found one, he reached down to tug at the emperor's mark in the center of the man's chest.

Then he snatched his fingers away as magic burned through the air.

"The chest plates!" Trulliç yelled at Bayzha. "We need to remove them!" He wasn't sure why the one he'd tried to touch had attacked him and burned his fingers. Maybe it was because it sensed another's magic.

The problem with using a wind was that it wasn't delicate. He couldn't tear the chest plate off without tearing a man to shreds. And he wasn't even sure he could touch the chest plates physically.

Bayzha came running toward him.

Before she got close, a spear flew out of air.

If Bayzha hadn't been running, with her back toward the rest of the line, she might have been able to catch the spear, or at least deflect it.

Instead, it caught her square in the middle of her back. Her arms flung out, as if she was trying to fly away. The spear's momentum carried her forward. She fell onto her face, looking like a pinned bird.

The three men from earlier came into sight. They saw Trulliç. Two immediately started shooting arrows toward him, while a third sent yet another spear.

Trulliç easily defended himself from their thrown attacks. He didn't let them come any closer, but blasted them again with strong winds.

This time they didn't get bowled over. They seemed ready, and caught each other before they fell further away.

The three of them remained locked together, two behind the first man.

His face grew terrible, as if it were made of wax and melted. His eyes burned with a brilliant gold fire. Fangs shot out of his mouth, already bloodied. His hands turned into great claws.

The man roared loud enough that Trulliç felt it in his bones. He found himself frozen with shock.

The creature, for he could no longer be called a man, gave a terrible, hypnotic cry as he started loping forward.

Trulliç shook and tried to free himself. There was something about the cry, something about the magic he'd just witnessed, that held him still.

The part of his mind not scrambling madly to free himself wondered briefly if this was what happened to the old kings, if the emperor had frozen them against their will.

The two men who'd been supporting the creature dropped to the desert ground, blackened husks, their life and all matter sucked away, not even their bones remained, just ashes.

Ashes. Dust. Sand.

While Trulliç couldn't move his limb at all, he could still call the sands and the winds.

He *blasted* the creature running at him.

As he expected, his attack didn't knock the thing off course.

But it did slow it down.

Trulliç refined his attack and sent out sands and tearing winds again. He couldn't levitate the creature away—like the cane, while Trulliç could see the creature, he could barely sense him. The monster's power was coming from someplace else, someplace that Trulliç couldn't reach. However, Trulliç could stop the transfer of power.

He focused on the scale burning bright in the center of the thing's chest, gathered his power together, then pushed out with all his might.

The heat of the sand rushing from him burned his fingers. It pushed back the *chafiyek* he wore over his hair. Nearby bodies crisped to ash all around him.

The great glob of glass that Trulliç had generated found its target. It smacked right into the creature's chest, hot enough to annihilate bone.

And, it seemed, strong enough to counter the emperor's magic.

The creature stopped. Trulliç heard the cry of a man this time, and not a beast. The liquid glass *burned* his chest, immolated the emperor's symbol.

The man cried again, dropping to his knees.

Now it was Trulliç's turn to run forward, trying to get to the man before he crumbled away.

The heated glob of glass smoldered on the remains of the man's chest. The emperor's symbol glowed brightly underneath it, as if trying to warn him away. Trulliç levitated the glass up, encasing the snake's scale.

Could he cut it completely off from the power of the emperor? It wasn't as strongly built as the head of the snake on the cane.

He added another layer of glass to the floating symbol, turning it in the air as he blew out and spun the glass. Green and gold stripes found their way into case, though Trulliç didn't knowingly add them.

The shape took on the form of a stylized heart, bulbous and full, containing the symbol of the emperor.

Trulliç felt the anger swirling from it. The emperor was trying to get at him, at his prize. He couldn't afford to be studied closely. Trulliç might learn too much.

The symbol stopped trying to suck at the magic surrounding it. Instead, power began to pour out of it.

Trulliç couldn't cut the leaf off from the emperor's power. They were too in tune with one another. Or maybe it was because this piece had come from the emperor directly, himself.

With a strong wind, Trulliç cast the encased symbol high into the air. The glass exploded as it reached the cooler temperatures up above him, shards and small spikes raining down.

Trulliç hadn't thought about dropping glass on his enemy like heavy rain, though he now realized he could do it, and could kill a large group that way.

But at least he finally had an idea how to stop the emperor from using the deaths of his soldiers to power himself. As well as a possible method for defeating the fighting army.

The star sisters needed to focus on the symbol of the emperor that every soldier wore. Would it be possible to tear the scale symbol off the fighting soldiers? Trulliç could tell his people to do the same. Without the emperor's symbol powering them, the soldiers might lose much of their training. Hell, maybe even half their strength.

They might become beatable.

After burying the bodies that remained and wiping the desert clean of their intrusion, Trulliç rose back up in the air.

His ragged army couldn't stop this group of soldiers from continuing. They'd all die trying.

However, he'd slowed this group down.

As Trulliç flew overhead, he gathered up his people, drawing up the wounded as well. The soldiers who remained didn't know where their enemy had disappeared to, or where they were going.

The soldiers would be delayed, but that was all, while they regrouped and tended to their own wounded.

Then they'd start their trek again.

Eventually, they'd reach Hayalevi.

CHAPTER SIX

NADEEM

NADEEM STOOD AT THE BACK of the gathering of the war council, listening to Trulliç's report. She'd seen the horrifyingly small number of the army who'd returned.

And Trulliç hadn't even been able to stop the soldiers attack, but merely to slow them down.

"Why didn't your border defenses stop them?" Levent asked.

Nadeem found herself nodding. She'd seen the glass ball rise up out of the desert and stop Magnus' group from crossing over to the sand.

"When I visited the city of Çandikili, the city's defenses didn't react to my presence," Trulliç said slowly. "I assumed at the time it was because I was such a minor threat. Now, I wonder if my magic was so strong it overwhelmed those defenses."

Nadeem heard the plain truth in Trulliç's voice. He wasn't bragging.

Breaking himself into a million pieces on the rugged rocks of Yalçin had truly changed him. The old Trulliç wouldn't have been able to admit to his own power.

"Could you have killed them all?" Aunt Parayat asked. "Once you located them?"

"Yes, but that wouldn't have been enough," Trulliç said adamantly. "If I drown them in sand, they'd explode out of it and taint the land. If I speared them with glass shards, the emperor would still have used their deaths to grow stronger. If I built a great glass wall around them, after they were dead, that would slow down the emperor, but not stop him. He and his men would keep coming."

"Maybe you can hold the men in sand, and the star sisters could then come and strip them of their emblem?" Seydat suggested.

"Maybe," Trulliç said slowly. "When I tried to pull the emperor's symbol from the chest of a fallen soldier, it burned my hands."

"We tried as well," said one of the star sisters who'd survived the battle. "It had the same effect. Couldn't touch it. We could carve the breast plate off the man, but it was like removing the hide from a goat. Magic seals the armor together. It won't come off easily."

Nadeem tried to pay attention to the rest of the questions, the ideas that everyone tossed into the ring. Trulliç could stop the armies at the border, but he couldn't stop the emperor. And he was wasting lives when he did so, lives that the emperor then fed on.

They could fight like this for years, with the emperor just sending troops into the desert, men willing to die on their own home soil. Though the desert was different enough from the rest of the empire that it probably felt foreign to them.

They had to bring the emperor here. While Trulliç could build a huge glass wall to keep the soldiers out, it also would keep all his people in. The desert people needed to trade with those outside the desert. Isolating themselves wouldn't work.

But how to bring the emperor here? Or at the very least, protect the people who already lived here?

She'd sworn to do everything in her power to stop the emperor from laying waste to all the lands. Trulliç had sworn a similar blood oath.

There had to be something more that she could do.

But what?

At the end of the evening meal, Nadeem helped Myrizhah gather up the dishes. Although Myrizhah could have directed anyone else to do it, she still insisted on doing it herself. "Gives my hands something to do," she said.

Nadeem understood that. It was why she'd volunteered to help. She needed to something, anything. The war council had come up with some new ideas, but Nadeem wasn't very hopeful.

Tomorrow would be another skirmish with the emperor's soldiers, probably the second prong of his attack.

And more would die.

Nadeem paused when she picked up the one plate that still contained a full serving of thick goat stew, with flatbread and tiny onions. Who hadn't eaten? Even Trulliç had taken a few bites, more to make the others comfortable than because he needed the food.

With a start, Nadeem realized that Myrizhah had set a full place for the goddess Barzhat. It was custom for the star sisters to do so: it was how they showed their love for the goddess, by including her in all the family meals, not just the feasts dedicated to her.

"Why did you set a place for the goddess Barzhat?" Nadeem asked as she followed the woman back into the large kitchen area.

Myrizhah shrugged. "I've done it often enough when I served star sisters, when I worked in the tavern," she said. "And we're preparing for more deaths. It seemed like the right thing to do. To invite the goddess here, to share bread with her, in the hopes that she'll judge our warriors lightly."

"Thank you," Nadeem said. It was a touching gesture.

It also gave her an idea.

"Where's Trulliç?" Nadeem asked as they finished rinsing off the plates.

"At the top of his tower, I'd imagine," Myrizhah said. "Studying the stars." She paused, she added, "He seems changed. More relaxed."

Nadeem paused, trying to figure out how best to explain it to his mother. "He went through a trial on Yalçin mountain," she said.

"Good," Myrizhah said, nodding. Then she speared Nadeem with a hard look. "May we all survive our own, individual trials."

Nadeem knew the woman was talking about Nadeem's issue, still living a half-life.

There wasn't anything she was willing to do about that, however. Not until after the war, though now, she very much doubted there would be an after the war for her.

Nadeem climbed to the top of the tower. She didn't bother announcing herself or knocking. Trulliç would have barred her from coming up if he didn't want to see her.

He stood at the far edge of the square opening, looking north over the desert. Riyune lay on the ground beside him, imitating a statue, with his front legs out and his back legs curled under him. The dog didn't even blink when Nadeem came up the stairs.

Stars filled the sky to over brimming. The air was cool up here, carrying the smells of roasting goat. She heard the murmur of the people below, a soft, soothing sound.

Trulliç turned as Nadeem crossed the space. He wore a simple muslin tunic striped with green and gold, his black-and-white checked *chafiyek* tied around his neck. He smiled sweetly at her. He kept his hands stiffly at his sides, though she knew he wanted to reach out and touch her.

Would she ever welcome his touch? Or even get used to it?

Nadeem walked silently to the edge of the tower and looked out. Night covered the desert, and the stars only showed a small slice of her beauty. Still, the sand appeared to sparkle, even from up here.

"I have an idea," Nadeem said quietly.

Trulliç turned to face the desert, seeming to understand that it was going to be easier for Nadeem to address it, and not him, directly.

"We—I mean the star sisters, welcome the goddess Barzhat into our lives and hearts," Nadeem said. "We are meant to love her, truly love her. To greet her with joy no matter what form she takes."

Trulliç nodded. He looked worried where this conversation was going. Nadeem continued anyway.

"In exchange, a sister can ask a single boon from the goddess, at the sister's time of greatest need," Nadeem said. "The goddess may or may not grant it. Usually she doesn't: the need is rarely great enough."

"Go on," Trulliç said, still looking worried.

"We are at our hour of greatest need," Nadeem said. "I plan to cross over to the myth lands and ask for Barzhat's help. Not just for fighting the soldiers, but to stop the emperor from taking the goddess' place."

"I see," Trulliç said. He sighed, as if a great weight had just settled onto his shoulders. "I don't want you to go," he said. "But I won't stop you, either."

"Thank you," Nadeem said. That was all she could ask for.

"And afterward?" Trulliç asked, his voice challenging. He turned now to face Nadeem. "What happens after the war if all is not lost?"

Nadeem nearly laughed. She should have known she couldn't talk to Trulliç without him bringing this up again.

"I will deal with you honestly, Trulliç," Nadeem said. She could promise him that. She took a deep breath. She'd felt fear a few times in her life, that fluttering feeling inside her chest that took her solid center away. She pushed it away, as she always did.

"I like you, Trulliç," Nadeem said softly. "I like the man you're becoming. So much more than the clueless boy who I always wanted to smack."

Trulliç chuckled and had the grace to look chagrined. "Good," he said. "I'm glad. However, I can hear a large 'but' coming."

"I go to embrace the goddess," Nadeem said. "Maybe to dance for her, to beg for her favor. Like your trial on the mountain, this will change me."

Trulliç nodded solemnly but held his tongue. He really was growing up.

"I don't know if there is any coming back from being with the goddess," Nadeem admitted. "I don't know what exactly will happen."

"I see," Trulliç said. "Though I don't, not really. No one knows what happens when we deal with the gods intimately."

He thought for a moment before he finally added, "Come back to me when you can. If you can. You will always have a place here."

"Thank you," Nadeem said. "Both for being willing to understand, as well as for the offer."

Trulliç gave her a crooked smile that made him look more rakish and less vulnerable. "Wherever you want to stand, here by my side, in my bed, or across the room, you will always be welcome."

Nadeem blinked, surprised. Trulliç was growing up. "I don't know what will be," she said softly. "I cannot make any promises. I will not be foresworn."

The silent word *again* echoed between them.

"Before you go then, let me apologize," Trulliç said.

"Whatever for?" Nadeem said, confused. What had he done that he felt the need to apologize?

"When we were in the myth lands. You were willing to sacrifice yourself to close the door to the desert heart," he said.

"Yes," Nadeem said. She still felt confused. There hadn't been any other choice.

"I didn't want to take your sacrifice," Trulliç said. "If I could have chosen myself, I would have. But you were right. The desert magician needed to live on, to fight the emperor."

"And?" Nadeem asked, her natural impatience building.

"I would have taken your life," he confessed in a small voice.

Nadeem snorted in derision. "There's nothing to forgive," she chided him. "We were both driven by need. I know you would have chosen differently if you'd had a chance."

"I just didn't want that standing between us," Trulliç said stubbornly. "I didn't want you to think I held you in less regard."

Nadeem shook her head. "You've been reading old love poems again, haven't you?"

Trulliç opened his mouth to deny it, but then closed it again. He shook his head and looked down at his feet.

Nadeem couldn't tell if he was blushing or not, not in the starlight.

"It's all right," she assured him gently. "I was ready to die."

"You still are," Trulliç said, his voice holding a harder edge.

"So are you," Nadeem shot back.

"I would, if that would save the desert," Trulliç said after a moment. "But I don't believe I'll be faced with that choice. I want to live. I want to have a life with you."

Nadeem held silence between them like a wall of glass. She would *not* respond, "Me too," as much as a part of her really wished to.

She had yet to embrace the goddess. Dance for the goddess of death.

The quiet of the desert surrounded Nadeem as she slowed. Stars cast an eerie glow on the sand. Maybe it only sparkled when Trulliç was there. She didn't hear even the rustling of wind, smoothing sand into ridged waves. The coolness of the night gave a dusty smell, making her think of places long forgotten.

There were still many hours before dawn. The night held its reign firmly.

Nadeem knew she was still on the edges of the ancient desert. She didn't have time, or Trulliç's speed, to get to the heart of the Qaenev. Still, she'd gotten to a place where man rarely traveled, as the caravans always came along the trade routes that outlined the sand.

Without hesitation, Nadeem pulled her obsidian knife from her belt. It had served her well in the past.

She'd already taken a blood oath to stop the emperor from desecrating the lands. Did she need to swear a new oath? Or just reaffirm the one she'd already taken?

Nadeem knelt on the cool sand. It felt solid under her legs, as though cast from hard stone. With a quick motion, she sliced open her left palm. Blood sprang up on either side of the peeling skin. Nadeem placed her hand down on the sand, ignoring the pain of the wound.

"I still stand by my oath to do everything in my power to stop the emperor from laying waste to these lands," Nadeem called out into the still air. "Now, my need is greater. I ask for the help of the gods to stop the emperor once and for all."

Though Nadeem didn't feel a great wind, she heard it swishing around her. She glanced to the side. Was something coming?

When she looked forward again, she saw the cavern immediately in front of her. The dark rocks still looked misshapen, piled haphazardly on top of one another. The opening felt as though it had been carved out of solid night, black and cold. She couldn't see through it to the guard stone.

Nadeem rose gracefully to her feet. She bowed her head low to the outcropping of rocks. "Thank you for coming," she said. She crossed the few feet necessary to reach the cavern, finally able to see inside. She paused before crossing the threshold, then deliberately reached across the opening and placed her still bleeding palm on the guard stone.

The coldness of the stone made her gasp. It hurt as well, sending shooting pains from her palm, circling her wrist, and up her arm.

Nadeem stubbornly refused to draw back, though. She gritted her teeth and kept pressing her weight against her palm.

Gradually, the pain decreased, until she felt as though she had a normal wound. When Nadeem pulled her hand away and looked at her palm, she couldn't help but gasp.

The skin had already closed and healed. However, the scar cut a wide swath across her palm, white and shiny even in the dark night.

Was this the last blood oath she'd ever take? Was that the significance of the large scar?

Or was it just the greatest one?

———

The cavern looked the same as it always had when Nadeem edged her way around the guard stone. The light from the stars outside gave enough light for her to see. A bubbling stream divided the cavern floor in two. Beyond, on the other side, were stone shelves for travelers to sleep on. She wondered why there were always four. Did the cavern never take more than that?

Grateful for the water, Nadeem knelt down beside the stream before she crossed it. First, she deliberately dipped her left palm into the water. A shock went across her palm, reminding her of rubbing against a wool blanket in winter then touching something else. She cupped her hand and took a deep drink. The water refreshed her and calmed her, like the first spring waters pouring off the mountains.

Then she splashed water on her cheek. The coldness made her gasp, but as always, the waters soothed the constant ache she felt, as if she'd applied a salve to the ravaged skin.

Would her cheek ever completely heal? She doubted it would. Magical desert sands kept the wound open. It never bled, and Trulliç had told her that it looked as though the skin had healed. Nadeem knew the truth, though she'd never tell Trulliç how much it hurt.

After standing and stretching, Nadeem stepped over the stream and lay down on the first stone shelf. She knew that for the cavern to move she had to pass into dreamtime. Fortunately, her years of training as a star sister had given her with the ability to fall asleep whenever she had the opportunity.

You never knew when the next time to sleep may come.

After a brief, timeless time, Nadeem woke. Even without turning her head she knew that the stars streamed across the sky outside. The cavern had taken her to the myth lands.

Though Nadeem didn't know how much time had passed, she still took the time to stretch, to prepare her limbs for great exertion. She didn't know what physical challenge she would face, but she assumed it would be daunting.

She was calling on a goddess, after all.

Refreshed from her nap and her time in the cavern, Nadeem stepped eagerly out into the cool desert night. The sand here sparkled, more than even when Nadeem stood with Trulliç, as if precious gems were scattered across her path. Stars streamed across the sky. Watching them, tracking them too closely, would make her dizzy. The air smelled sweet, as if a caravan carrying incense had just passed.

Without traveling there to make certain, Nadeem still knew exactly which direction lay the cave that held Forit's heart. She was equally sure that wasn't where she needed to go. The goddess Barzhat, while being the judge of death, wasn't going to found close to where Forit had made her greatest sacrifice.

Nadeem turned her back and walked the opposite direction. She didn't know if it was correct, but she had to go somewhere, now that she was here in the myth lands.

How would she know when she'd arrived at the right place? Was there a temple dedicated to Barzhat here in the desert?

No, there wouldn't be. Barzhat's golden court lay under the sea, not the sand.

Still, Nadeem marched in the direction she felt was north, trying to find the right spot, a place that felt appropriate, that she could dedicate to the goddess.

Nadeem didn't have to travel very far. Or at least it didn't feel like she'd traveled a long way from the cavern, though when she looked over her shoulder, she couldn't see it.

Dunes of sand rose up on either side of her, creating a natural bowl. The ground felt more smooth here, like the fine sand of a performance space. Nadeem walked to the center of the impression and turned around. Behind her, another dune blocked her sight. When she turned forward again, she realized that only a small path led the way out of the depression.

It was like a circular arena, with a single way out.

Or like a trap.

Still, this felt like the right place.

Nadeem stood in the exact center and sang out one of the star sisters' usual greetings to Barzhat:

O great goddess! We welcome you!
Come partake of our hospitality!
Your place is with us
At the heart of our gathering
O great goddess! Please join us!
You are always welcome
In whatever form you may take
At the heart of our family!
O great goddess! Our love knows no bounds!
We will always clamor for your return
Please sup with us
Your place is always ready

Nadeem paused and listened after she finished. She didn't hear any response, no winds suddenly sprang up, the goddess' tinkling anklets didn't sound in the air.

She should have known it wouldn't be as easy as that.

As part of her training, Nadeem had learned dances to the goddess, practice for when you arrived in her golden court. She started off with a few steps of that, but stopped herself after only a few moments.

That wasn't right either. Those steps were too fancy, too prepared. The goddess needed Nadeem to dance from her heart.

There had been a training sequence that Nadeem had learned. It was a series of blocks, jabs, punches, and kicks. It felt more appropriate to her, a dance of death.

Nadeem started by placing her palms together and bowing her head to the north, the direction of the goddess. Then she started deliberately moving. First a slow block with one arm, followed by an equally slow punch with the other. Step, step, low block and pivot. Sweeping kick, heel kick, block, block, block.

By the time Nadeem finished the sequence, she found herself sweating, even in the cool night air.

The goddess hadn't come. But Nadeem felt as though she was on the right track.

She went through the fight sequence again, moving with a fraction more speed. Then again. And again. Her dance of death sent her hands flying, her feet kicking, her body swaying as she blocked unseen opponents.

She couldn't add magical speed to her dance. Though this place resembled the Qaenev desert, it wasn't, not really. The myth lands demanded that a person be just as they were, without special abilities or really, even magic.

Still, Nadeem had been training for long enough that she was able to almost move at a blur as she danced and sweat freely under the streaming skies.

A shuffling sound filled the area. Nadeem didn't break her dance, but let it carry her naturally around.

A dark figure had appeared on the edge of the bowl, seated, as if watching a performance.

Nadeem's heart was already racing with the effort of her dance. She still felt it lurch, and her breath grew short.

Was that the goddess? Had Nadeem been blessed with her presence?

Then a second figure appeared. And a third.

No, it wasn't the goddess. Nadeem danced on. Fear fluttered around the edges of her skin. Were these warriors that the goddess would make her fight? They were darkly clothed, like star sisters.

How close would death come this time for Nadeem? Would she finally step fully into its sweet embrace?

More figures filled the arena, silently watching. What were they waiting for?

While the desert gave Nadeem great power, she still knew that she would falter before long. She was still human, and she couldn't dance forever. Not like she would when she finally came to dance in the real court of the goddess.

Finally, Nadeem stumbled after a kick, her legs too tired to draw back fully and place her foot properly. All the exhaustion that Nadeem had tried to forget came slamming down on her, weighing her down as heavily as one the goddess' teardrop-shaped weights would after Nadeem died. She still struggled on, throwing yet another punch, then doing a sweep with her legs.

No, wait. That was the wrong place. She'd skipped ahead.

Where should she start? She turned and blocked again, but then couldn't remember what followed next.

She was going to have to start from the beginning, at that slow place.

A bell rang out, clear through the night air, as if signaling the end of a match.

Nadeem froze where she stood, though she panted heavily. Sweat covered her skin. She blinked, trying to clear her vision.

A whirlwind of blue sand stood at the only opening to the bowl-shaped depression where Nadeem had been dancing. Was that the goddess? Nadeem stared, trying to make out the goddess' two faces, one blue, one black, or even her four arms. Some of the paintings and statues showed Barzhat with twelve legs, though Nadeem had always imagined the goddess with merely two.

Streaks of lightning went out from the sandstorm. They buzzed by Nadeem, making all the hair on the back of her neck stand up, as well as the hair along her arms. The bolts struck the figures sitting there, passively watching like stones.

Nadeem shivered as the first stirred, as though waking. The darkness shrouding the figure dissolved. Nadeem found herself looking at a star sister, her cheek proudly marked for all to see. She wore a sleeveless black tunic tied tightly around her waist, tight black stretchy leggings that would allow her to move, as well as heavy black sandals.

The only color on the woman was the great golden teardrop that appeared attached to the front of her tunic.

Nadeem turned back to the whirling sand storm in front of her. "Who are these women?" she asked out loud. Her voice sounded tinny in the night air.

The women themselves answered her. "We are star sisters, long deceased." The chorus of their voices barely sounded above the shifting sand. "We have one last dance for the goddess before we are reborn."

Nadeem suddenly understood. The golden teardrop each woman wore was the last weight given to them by the goddess, the last deed they needed to atone for before the goddess would grant them true death. The women would fight the soldiers of the emperor until the goddess judged that they were worthy. Then, the teardrop would fall from their bodies and they would disappear to be reborn elsewhere.

"Thank you," Nadeem said, addressing the whirlwind that was slowly fading. "I am forever in your debt. I will always welcome you with a warm embrace."

Was that laughter she heard in reply? The goddess seemed happy to accept her gift.

Nadeem turned to address the dark forms seated around her. "Thank you, star sisters, for giving the people of the desert your last dance."

A murmur went up among the women. Had they only now realized that Nadeem wasn't really a star sister?

One of the figures suddenly sprang up beside Nadeem. Though she was merely a shade, Nadeem could still tell that she'd at one point been one of the desert people, due to her darker skin, large nose, and tight curls that fell around her face.

The figure held out her hand. Across her palm lay one of the golden teardrops of the goddess.

"Take this," came the whispered command.

Unwelcome fear spiked through Nadeem. She wanted to refuse. She didn't want to touch this weight, to bring her own time dancing before the goddess any closer.

But she'd come this far. She'd sworn to do everything she could, and with the help of the goddess, maybe she could stop the emperor.

With a steady hand, Nadeem reached out to lift the weight from the star sister's palm.

The cold of it burned her fingers, burning away what life Nadeem had felt. She shivered, but she didn't drop it. Instead, she took the weight and pressed it against her own chest, saying, "I gladly embrace you, Barzhat."

Ice shot through her blood, freezing her solid. The world took a step back, and Nadeem felt as though she watched everything again from a distance.

She had been taking steps, albeit small one, back toward the land of the living.

Now, she'd gone back to the world of the dead, to the half-life she'd had before.

Trulliç was going to be well and truly angry, despite the help she brought.

It was too late. Nadeem had asked the goddess for help. And Barzhat had indeed given her a great boon.

Now, Nadeem just had to pay the price.

CHAPTER SEVEN

TRULLIÇ

TRULLIÇ CONTAINED HIS ANGER, THOUGH he wanted to rage and storm across the face of the desert when Nadeem returned.

Yes, it was marvelous that the goddess had decided to help, gifting them with the shades of star sisters. Trulliç didn't know what their abilities would be, but he assumed they'd easily be the match of any of the emperor's special soldiers.

But the price…He didn't want to pay the price of Nadeem's soul.

He didn't have any choice. The decision had been hers, as it always had been.

Instead of raging, Trulliç thanked Nadeem profusely: polite, formal words that expressed at least some of his relief. Then, instead of disappearing back into his tower as he wanted, he remained on the ground level, listening to the latest battle plans as they were being formed by the war council.

"We know that the emperor will strike again soon," Levent said. "Possibly today. But where?"

"Midway between Egreliki and Gaadiwala?" Trulliç guessed. "Just south of Çandikili, to the west?" The attack against Egreliki wouldn't happen until the next day, it made sense that the emperor would split the difference between where he'd sent his first line of soldiers and the third.

Trulliç hadn't gone to check on the survivors of Gaadiwala, if there were any. He knew it was partly out of cowardice, as they'd be right to blame him for the fate that had fallen on their heads, as undeservedly as it might have been. He hoped he could help the villagers after the war, but he couldn't focus on them right now, as much as he might want to. Plus, there was only so much he could do for people outside of his land.

He hated this pressure of time. It felt so unnatural, not how the desert moved at all.

"He might attack there," Aunt Parayat said, nodding. It was obvious she knew the geography of the Tanesh Empire and didn't need to consult a map. "His men could also be coming on ships, and attack closer to Nusaybil Valley, which would be closer to Hayalevi as well."

Was that what Zehra had meant by the emperor crashing on his shores? Or was it that the emperor would strike out at Egreliki from the ocean, instead of overland?

"The main city of the emperor, Atayurtkah, is north and slightly east of Gaadiwala," Trulliç said. If he sent his out his troops from the main city at the same time, one could have marched directly to Gaadiwala, while the other could have gone to the coast, and sailed down the coast from there."

"That actually makes more sense," Aunt Parayat said. "Particularly if the emperor did send men from the main city."

"Where would he stop at Nusaybil Valley? Why not sail directly to further down the coast to the port that's closest to Hayalevi?" Seydat asked.

"He'd be able to pick up more star sisters near Nusaybil," Aunt Parayat said. "More trained troops."

That froze Trulliç's soul. The first group hadn't contained any star sisters, just soldiers. He didn't want to set sister against sister.

He had no choice. The ones fighting for the emperor had chosen the wrong side, that of a mere man intent on overthrowing their goddess.

"I think we can all agree that the emperor's sent men along the coast, and is expecting to land as close to Hayalevi as he can," Myrizhah said, looking around the war council.

"Then why attack at the top of the Qaenev desert first?" Trulliç asked, confused.

"To get you to spend men and energy," Levent replied. "The emperor, for all his power, isn't a land magician. It's difficult for him to do what you do in terms of logistics. And he's never had to fight anyone with so much land or power."

"He still killed so many of my people," Trulliç said. He felt his cheeks grow darker, flaring with rage. He was able to control his anger so much better than before, however, the deaths from earlier made him truly upset.

"I'm sorry you lost so many good men," Levent said softly. "But we gained so much knowledge from that first battle!"

"The emperor gained knowledge as well," Trulliç pointed out.

"He didn't learn the full extent of your power," Aunt Parayat said flatly. "You've yet to show that."

Trulliç blinked, surprised. While on the one hand, he had been holding himself back, on the other, surely the emperor already knew? Then again, had the emperor ever dealt with a true desert magician before? Maybe that hadn't been the power of the six kings...

"It was good that the emperor was able to overcome your defenses near Gaadiwala," Levent said with a sharp nod. "Let's make sure that the continues to underestimate you."

"No," Trulliç said, the power in his voice surprising even to him. "If the emperor continues to just send his men to die and bleed my people, I'll never be able to win, or to defeat him. We will only end this war when we end the emperor."

The uneasy silence around the room made Trulliç shiver. Did they all think he'd fail when he faced the emperor?

"You can't attack the emperor," Aunt Parayat said, pointing out the obvious. "His cloak protects him from you. From all the star sisters as well."

Trulliç shrugged. "The emperor won't be in his court when he comes to Qaenev. He'll be in the desert. And he'll finally face the full power of the desert magician."

"Do you really think you'll win?" Myrizhah asked.

Trulliç wasn't certain if that was wonder he heard in her voice. "This is my land," Trulliç said, keeping his tone low. "I won't let anyone take it from me."

Hadn't he expressed that clearly before? Evidentially not, based by the rustle that went through the room. Even Riyune looked up, as if surprised.

"Then we should plan on a fourth attack," Aunt Parayat said, her words cutting through the unease. "The second will occur possibly after Egreliki, closer to Hayalevi. After both are crushed, the emperor may grace us with his presence. We should be prepared for such an honored guest."

Trulliç nodded, truly impressed by the amount of sarcasm the older woman managed to drip through her words.

Would he really have a day's rest between attacks?

Or, as he'd feared, would the next attack, so close to Hayalevi, mean that he couldn't split his army, and therefore would have to choose to let Egreliki fall?

T he entire city waited restless as time passed and the next attack didn't come. The troops were gathered and told to stay near the gather point, so that Trulliç could easily fling them into harm's way.

Sunlight burned bright in the mid-afternoon. Most people napped, or at least tried to, under what shade they could create. Trulliç blew cool breezes over them, though he couldn't sweeten their dreams.

Relief and dread came with the falling of night. Maybe they would have one more day to live. Or maybe the emperor would attack at midnight, when Trulliç's powers were at their weakness.

Many of those waiting spent the early part of the evening singing. Some even performed ritual dances, practicing for their meeting with Barzhat.

Trulliç went with Nadeem out beyond Barzhat's temple, just north of the city, where the true desert began again. The stars shone down coldly over the glittering sand. Trulliç's soft heart was intent on breaking as Nadeem walked silently beside him, not sharing words with him. She'd grown so silent, *as silent as a grave* his poet's heart pointed out.

How could he bring her back to him?

Nadeem stopped at the top of a small rise. She pressed one hand against her chest, where the golden tear-drop of the goddess had nestled beneath her skin.

Trulliç winced at how pressing against her chest appeared to hurt her, though she would never have complained. (Just as she never complained about the wound in her cheek, though Trulliç knew it still bothered her as well.)

With her other hand, Nadeem reached out into the darkness. She made a fist, and pulled, the muscles of her arm straining.

Dark shapes popped up above the sand, growing like misbegotten shadows.

"Star sisters," Nadeem said, as if she was explaining to Trulliç what he saw. "The emperor has not yet come. Tomorrow you will be called to your task, by the desert magician. Obey him as you would me."

Trulliç blinked, startled. Why would she have to say that? Or were the star sisters likely to not listen to him?

"Thank you," Trulliç said, first to Nadeem, then to the gathered crowd of shades before him. "You will get to do great deeds tomorrow, defending the desert from invaders."

A soft sigh went through the crowd, as if relieved to find out their task.

"Is it possible to send them to Egreliki?" Trulliç asked Nadeem as they walked back toward Hayalevi, the spirits all gone back to their resting places.

"I don't think that's wise," Nadeem answered slowly. "It's better for them to stay here and defend the city. Particularly if Aunt Parayat is right, and the emperor stopped in Nusaybil Valley."

"Can't the star sisters here take care of them?" Trulliç asked. He wanted to be able to save the shining jewel of a city.

"I wouldn't ask them to," Nadeem said firmly. "They have enough to deal with, fighting against the emperor. They shouldn't have to fight their own sisters as well."

Trulliç sighed, defeated. She was right. It wasn't fair of him to ask the star sisters to fight their own. Not the living ones, at any rate.

"Then I will send more star sisters with the army going north, to Egreliki," Trulliç said.

Nadeem shrugged. "You're sending them to their death, either way."

Trulliç couldn't help but shiver at the coldness in her voice. "Then they'll be able to fulfill their greatest duty, won't they?" he asked, unable to hide the bitterness he felt.

"Yes," Nadeem said, replying very seriously. "Exactly."

Obviously, she didn't understand that there could possibly be anything wrong with that.

The old Nadeem would have.

Trulliç woke with the dawn, as usual. He made himself smile, though he knew that Atça would have smacked him for being so fanciful, believing that he could feel the first of the sun's rays as they struck the desert.

Atça had just been so wrong about so many things.

Trulliç sighed as he stretched his arms above his head, then gave a great yawn. He'd not slept properly all night, but merely dozed, dipping into sleep between dreams of violence and chaos.

Atça was no longer worth his time. Trulliç could already feel the place where his mentor had once ruled with an iron fist dwindling.

It was good.

Trulliç looked down, finding Riyune there, as he expected. The ghost dog didn't climb up and share heat as often as the old dog had.

Or maybe he, too, had had a restless night, given the yawn Riyune now returned.

"Come," Trulliç said, standing. He quickly shed his sleeping tunic, putting on a nicely made off-white shirt that fit him perfectly across the shoulders, along with a sturdy pair of brown trousers.

Myrizhah had shaken her head at his request, but she'd gone ahead and cleaned the tunic he'd worn for his manhood journey, a symbol to remind him of how far he'd come. The tunic only came down to the tops of his thighs now, instead of hanging down to his knees. It still looked new, though the linen was no longer stiff, the gold and green stripes looked fresh: the pale gold of the desert at first light mixed with the light green of the hills at the start of the rainy season.

Trulliç didn't go downstairs to meet with the war council who had probably already started to gather. Instead, he went up to the open top of the tower, to bathe in the sunlight himself.

He felt himself grow stronger in the light, breathing in the dry scents of the desert mingled with the smoke of the cooking fires down below. He walked to the north-eastern edge this time, casting his senses out, seeking the first of the emperor's attack.

For a brief moment, he thought he caught something. It was as light as a leaf blowing across a fence, to land in a neighbor's yard before being quickly swept up.

He knew better than to think he'd imagined it.

Instead, Trulliç focused all his attention in that direction, seeking something, anything, that felt out of place.

The desert felt empty, though. He could sense a caravan up the main trade route, a little to the north.

Were these guards who were hiding? Or had he just been fooled?

Trulliç would go greet the council, then take a trip out to the border to make sure.

He was halfway across the open space, heading toward the stairs, when he felt the eastern border come alive.

The soldiers were here.

T rulliç raced down the stairs and out the tower. There wasn't any more deliberation the council could do now. It was finally time to act. He flew over the sands to where his people had gathered. Many were just waking up, not ready to fight.

The star sisters saw his expression and knew, whether their charges were ready to go or not.

Loud hooting horns rang through camp. As they had practiced, people dropped whatever else they were holding and picked up their weapons. As one, they turned to face the east.

Trulliç swallowed around a dry throat. Many of these people were going to be killed today.

He would honor each and every one of their sacrifices the rest of his life.

"To arms! To arms!" came the unnecessary human call.

Nadeem appeared beside Trulliç. So did Riyune.

Levent came up quickly as well. He was dressed as a soldier for the first time. Trulliç couldn't afford to supply all his combatants with the fancy leather breast plates the emperor used. Instead, everyone had to buy their own.

Levent had worked a deal with a couple of leather merchants, who'd come up with their own version of a square badge, striped green and gold, that he wore proudly on one bicep. He had his own leather vest, with square pieces of leather, staggered in rows, brigandine style. A thick leather apron covered the tops of his legs. It looked as though it had come from a local smith, streaked with black coal. He had his own shield strapped to one arm, a tall wooden piece shaped like an arrowhead and rimmed with brass. He carried a sword in the other hand, curved like the men of the south.

Around his neck he wore a glass amulet, given to him by Trulliç.

If there were to be any poems about today, Trulliç would start with Levent, standing brave and proud in mismatched armor, about to lead a horde instead of a well-trained unit.

Trulliç didn't take the time to talk to his company. They knew what they were up against. They knew the odds of survival.

They also knew that every man they killed would make the enemy stronger. So many of them carried ropes cut to short lengths to tie men up, or blunted swords.

Trulliç didn't trust the gleam in Nadeem's eye, as if she relished the upcoming brush with death. Hopefully she wouldn't fully embrace the goddess. Not yet.

With his head raised toward the sun like a flower, Trulliç gathered all his people together. He tasted the cool glass they all carried. He gave each piece a small boost of power, hoping to protect these souls. They rose like a great storm and flew off quickly toward the eastern horizon.

The journey wasn't very far, just over a day's travel for a caravan.

However, the sight at the border gladdened his heart.

The emperor *had* underestimated Trulliç.

First off, the emperor had sailed his men down closer to Hayalevi to bring the fight here, rather than stop at Nusaybil to pick up a large contingent of star sisters.

And second, while the enemy soldiers were still far too many men to count, they were stymied at the border.

Hundreds of glass balls had risen out of the sand when the soldiers had tried to cross the border. The balls were arrayed on either side of the main column, as thick as a three foot wall. The balls were myriad sizes: some as small as a man's eye, while others were as bigger than a man's head. They floated at different levels in front of the soldiers, constantly shifting and threatening.

Trulliç deposited his army down on the desert side of the balls. "Check for star sisters slipping around the sides," he quietly instructed Levent before turning to slowly walk up to where the defenses stood. This also gave Levent and the others time to arrange themselves, getting ready to battle.

"How dare you challenge the emperor and his envoy!" a harsh voice called out as Trulliç drew near.

"You are no envoy," Trulliç countered. "You are an attacking force. If you came in peace, you wouldn't have disturbed my defenses."

It was mostly true. Only those with death in their hearts bothered the glass balls. Though the star sisters had rarely caused them to rise up, as they lived too closely to death.

"Let us through, so that we might negotiate," the soldier said.

Trulliç finally identified the man. Like Marius, he was shorter than the soldiers around him. He stood on bowed legs, his skin as dark as the desert people. However, he also had the features of the men from Lydae, with lighter eyes and hair.

"Negotiate what?" Trulliç asked. He knew these people were here to attack. What would they try to bargain for first?

"Your surrender!" the man said. He started laughing and the soldiers nearest him also chuckled, as if he'd just told a joke.

Trulliç stepped back. "No," he said firmly. "The desert is mine. The emperor will have to come and take it from me himself if he wants it."

The soldiers seemed a little unsure about that. Maybe the emperor had assured them that Trulliç would be no threat.

How little they knew.

Riyune, who'd grown huge again, gave a warning growl. The soldiers closest to the dog paled.

The lead man looked to his left and his right, before turning back to Trulliç. "All right," he said, sounding easy going as he strapped his shield to one arm, then unsheathed his sword. "But it will be your widows mourning tonight, not ours."

He raised his sword and called out, "Attack! Attack!"

The call was taken up by others up and down the line.

Trulliç kept his ground though he trembled inside.

They were coming for him.

The glass balls quickly flew toward the soldiers running across the border. The men ended up swinging their swords wildly in the air as the glass balls attacked their heads. More than one soldier ended up injuring his neighbor as the glass balls swooped and turned.

As the balls got through the men's defenses, the soldiers started dropping to the ground, usually unconscious. If a soldier managed a lucky strike, the glass exploded, casting sharp slivers and slicing through the skin and armor of all the men nearby, some of which were fatal.

A group of more than two dozen men seemed determined to cut through all the balls to get to Trulliç. He kept retreating as he'd been instructed by Nadeem. His heart beat as hard as if he was doing all the fighting. He'd never been attacked this way, that slow pace backwards, as if treading through thick sand in a nightmare.

He suddenly appreciated what little wrestling training Nadeem had given him, trying to teach him how to be calm in a battle. He knew he'd never reach her expertise, but at least he could try.

Riyune had left his side, going to harry the invaders. His great speed startled them, and he crushed more than one with his weight.

He rarely bit, though Trulliç did see him take out the throat of a soldier who wouldn't turn away from Trulliç.

However, there were more men than defensive balls, something Trulliç had already known. He'd scattered the glass balls heavily up and down the battle line, leaving fewer to defend himself, hoping to protect his people.

Though the group focused on him had been halved, that still left over a dozen men on his trail. They each had the emperor's symbol glowing brightly in the center of their leather breastplates. They moved as a unit, connected through the emperor's magic. At least they were still running, and not flying.

Fortunately, the soldiers fighting Trulliç's people weren't part of the emperor's elite, and were more like regular men. This gave Trulliç's people more of a chance.

Finally, when the last of the glass balls dropped away, Trulliç stopped and stamped the ground with his foot. "Now!" he called. "I call on the shades of the star sisters to attack!"

Shadows rose all around him. They flowed toward the emperor's men like a dark wave.

The collision was silent, the men's voices already stolen from them by the dead.

The soldiers fought bravely. Trulliç would have to grant them that. They didn't freeze or run in fear. They stayed and tried to kill the dead, those dark souls who'd come for theirs.

As Trulliç watched, a few of the dark sisters lost the golden teardrop attached to their chest. Had they performed their final dance? Or had the emperor somehow reached out and sucked up what power remained to them?

Trulliç hoped they would manage to be reborn, leaving the goddess' court for good.

When the last man died, Trulliç turned his attention to the rest of the battle.

He didn't like what he saw.

Close to him, the battle raged fiercely. Clanging swords, grunting men, and the occasional breaking of bones filled his ears. The smell of gore washed over him, as awful as the first time. His stomach churned. He sent his winds, knocking away the foes, bowling them down so his people could disarm them.

Trulliç hurried up the line first, sinking soldiers to their knees in sand, blowing them over, and blinding them. He sent massive bolts of power through the linked groups, overwhelming their connection. The men fell apart and succumbed to the next wave from his people.

Past the line of soldiers, the star sisters fought, the dead with the living. Odd illusions wove in and out of the battling sisters, fantastic hawkmen, lithe goat women, and others.

Nadeem had told him of the great illusionary battles she'd once fought, partly as a precaution so the sisters wouldn't accidentally injure or kill each other. Maybe the old habits were deeply ingrained, so the attackers kept returning to their illusions.

Or perhaps the illusions fooled the shades, as he saw more than one of the dead star sisters fighting an illusion, and not a physical foe.

Trulliç changed the ground under the feet of the star sisters, making the sand more slippery. It seemed to help. There wasn't much more he could do for them, however. While he disliked the emperor's soldiers, he felt bad killing the star sisters.

As his mother would say, his soft heart would always get him in trouble.

Trulliç turned and went back down the line, striking down foes where he could. He wasn't surprised to find that at least half the fallen soldiers were now bare chested. Whenever he found a breastplate beside a body, he cast it over the border. Let the emperor reclaim them there. He didn't want that foul magic in his kingdom.

Further down the line, Trulliç found Levent fighting. He gracefully slaughtered those who came to attack, his sword in constant motion, dancing to the right and left, twirling and punching. His face was covered in sweat in dirt, and blood spattered his leather armor.

The soldiers who came after him were the best. Trulliç aimed his winds carefully, trying to blow them away without striking Levent as well.

But he didn't aim well enough. A soldier stepped left, into the force, just as Trulliç started. The man got blown against Levent, instead of away from him.

Before Trulliç could cast another wind, the man whirled and struck Levent, hitting his head hard enough that he dropped to his knees.

With a mighty *whoosh*, Trulliç swept away all those who were near, friend and foe alike. He hurried over and helped Levent rise up.

"Fool," Levent said through gritted teeth. "I had them."

Stung, Trulliç stepped back. "I was just trying to help."

"Go help those who need it," Levent said, shaking his head before leaping back into the fray.

"I will," Trulliç said, turning away. He really had been trying to help. He blasted the next soldiers who came near at least thirty feet in the air, dropping their broken bodies down onto the sand. Then he called up more glass, hurling molten balls at any who dared come near.

Trulliç heard the arrows before he saw them. He instinctively raised up a great glass globe around himself. The arrows dinged off the glass, sounding like winter hail. The cries of those outside of the globe were terrible to hear.

Trulliç rose up into the air, above the next barrage of arrows, leaving those on the ground safely ensconced. Where were those archers?

There. Off in the distance. They stood behind a massive group of soldiers, all shielded. No one could reach the group.

Trulliç didn't bother getting closer. Instead, he sank the archers far into the sand, up to their chests. Those standing with shields started to sink as well.

"He's in the air!" came a loud cry.

A few of the archers had been hiding behind the main group, out of the way. They instantly shot arrows up at Trulliç.

Did they really think that mere arrows were going to hurt him? Or was this another feint?

Trulliç turned his well-protected back on the archers just in time. A third group crept up behind him, intending to skewer him from behind.

"Blast all of you!" Trulliç said, growing angrier. Instead of glass globes he cast molten glass down on the group, burning the men alive. He made himself listen to their screams, not taking himself away.

He'd done that. He'd killed them. He could listen to them die.

The group who remained, Trulliç buried up to their necks in sand. They couldn't dig themselves out, couldn't escape. He knew his people could take care of them, knock them unconscious then dig them out and disarm them. He'd have to come back later to cast the armor aside.

When Trulliç returned to the main line, most of the fighting was over. His people had won this battle, but at a great cost to themselves.

Still, the stragglers cheered as they saw Trulliç. The few star sisters who'd fought for the emperor had been all disarmed as well. Trulliç let Nadeem and the others deal with them.

It took Trulliç a moment to realize that Levent hadn't made it. Had he been too injured from Trulliç's mistake? Too angry? Trulliç would never forget how graceful the man moved in battle during his last few moments.

Trulliç would have to write a poem about him someday, once all the battles were over.

Trulliç had just gathered his people together, getting them ready to go back to Hayalevi, when he felt the start of the next incursion in Egreliki.

More troops had come.

He hurried as fast as he could, racing with the dead and the wounded back to Hayalevi. At least the sun remained high, powering him.

"To me! To me!" he called as soon as he set foot in Hayalevi.

The star sisters came rushing out. The loud ram's horns sounded again. A second group of citizens formed, this time, all facing the northwest.

Riyune ran up to Trulliç as the group formed. The dog seemed unaffected by the previous battle, though blood still stained his muzzle. Nadeem came up to stand on his other side. Streaks of dried blood ran down her face. The star sisters who'd survived the first battle came up and joined her.

The group of people behind Trulliç swelled. Many of the desert people from the second battle had joined them.

Trulliç wanted to turn down their help, to tell them to stay in Hayalevi. They'd seen enough killing for one day.

But he couldn't. He needed them, all of them. He would be forever in their debt.

He closed his eyes briefly, refreshing himself with the deep, dusty smell of the desert.

Then it was time for the next battle.

CHAPTER EIGHT

NADEEM

NADEEM REMEMBERED HER DANCE FOR the goddess, how slow it had started and then how quickly it had progressed.

The battle at Egreliki had some of the same qualities. It took Trulliç more time than she expected to send them flying over the desert. Then again, he was tired, having already fought a battle that day, casting more magic than she'd ever seen him do before. Also, Egreliki was much farther away from Hayalevi than the first battleground.

Once they touched down, Nadeem felt herself speeding up. She enjoyed the dance, the thrusting, blocking, punching and kicking. She fought with her bare hands mostly, feeling as though the goddess had turned her entire body into a weapon, able to kill with divine grace.

The shadow sisters moved with her. She fought at their side. The emperor's specially trained guards were their primary target, as this group of invaders had no star sisters with them. The men, however, had the touch of the emperor, his magic seeping from their chests like yellow pus.

Nadeem breathed in the scent of sweat, her own and the soldiers in front of her. Their leather smelled too, of dust and long days. The smell of the emperor's magic reminded Nadeem of a funeral pyre, that sickly sweet smell that came from burning flesh.

Her feet found the earth easily, never stumbling on the desert sand. It grounded her, reminding her of where she'd come from, where she was going. She'd always been a desert creature, shifting and flowing with the wind.

With her hands, she found her enemies. They fought with swords, foolishly thinking that bit of steel might save them. She used her knife on occasion, when a neck presented itself, or a bare arm. Usually, though, she just used her hands to break noses, collar bones, arms, wrists, or necks.

She kicked too, breaking legs, though that wasn't as common. Leg bones were much more difficult to break. Much easier to sweep a man's feet out from under him, then jump on his chest to break his ribs, or kick him unconscious.

Through the length of the battle, Nadeem felt as though she floated in the embrace of the goddess. She didn't feel sorry for the men she killed. She wasn't angry at them, either, though she knew that Trulliç was upset at the deaths these men had committed, killing the pretty Zahra and leaving her broken body in the middle of the street.

Everything stayed at a comfortable distance.

The only time Nadeem had any qualms was when one of her shadow sisters passed, not through fulfilling her duty, but because one of the emperor's men got ahold of her golden teardrop and sucked the animating force out of her.

Nadeem wasn't exactly sure how they were doing it. She suspected it was the emperor himself operating through the men, particularly given how their eyes burned and their tongues lolled out of their mouths.

She took extra care to kill those men. And possibly not as swiftly.

A group of them had surrounded one of the shadow sisters. She fought beautifully, but there were just too many of them, sucking at her strength.

Of course, it would take six of them to take down a single star sister.

Nadeem came up from behind. Her black blade, the one shaped like a long *meslit* thorn, found her hand. She sliced through the armor of one of the men from behind, stabbing his kidneys and dropping him where he stood. The next, she sliced open the artery in his neck, blood spurting everywhere.

However, then the men turned away from the shadow sister and toward her. The deaths of their companions had seemed to enrage them more.

Belatedly, Nadeem recalled how the emperor lived on death, and his men were likely to do the same. Trulliç had told her. She hadn't remembered, though. It wasn't important to the goddess.

Too late now.

Nadeem fought. Blades found both her hands as she whirled, planting them in necks and sliding hides. Kicks found their targets as well, the soft parts of the body, like elbows and knees. The shadow sister tried to help, but she'd been drained by the men. Her eyes were lifeless, like black holes.

When only two remained, Nadeem found that she'd been cut. Blood flowed along her right arm. She didn't feel the pain. Knew she wouldn't, not until long after the battle.

After the battle. After the war.

Something lurched in Nadeem, possibly her frozen heart. For a moment, she stood on the battlefield with all her senses woken: the coppery smell of blood and iron, the panting of her own breath, the terrible sounds of dying all around her, how sore her bare feet were, covered in bruises, like her hands.

And these men were trying to kill her.

Nadeem growled as she sprang back into action. She forced her feet to move twice as fast as they had been. She was a desert creature. They men were monsters, here to despoil the quiet places, tear down the oasis, spoil the dates and sweet marsh plants that held in the water.

These were the men who marked the cheeks of the star sisters, forcing them into a singular life.

These were the men who had killed her people and her peace of mind.

Nadeem became a whirlwind between them, slicing them to ribbons.

When they'd both fallen, she found Trulliç standing next to her. She didn't cut him, though it was a close call, as she'd mistaken him for an enemy at first.

"I thought I'd lost you," he said.

Or she thought that was what he'd said. Her ears seemed blocked by sand.

"Not yet," she assured him. She felt her face break into a grin. The movement felt strange, as if she hadn't smiled for a long while.

Then the goddess swept her up in her embrace again, and Nadeem rejoined the dance of killing.

Nadeem fought desperately. The soldiers kept *coming*. It was as if more boats had pulled onto the shore and they'd raced from the piers and poured into the village of Egreliki. It surprised her that those pretty white walls hadn't been painted red with blood, given the number they'd killed.

Despite how the goddess had sustained her, Nadeem still knew she was fading. She moved with speed and diligence, striking down all those who would despoil her. But her feet no longer had the punch they once did. This last man didn't go down after she successfully kicked his knee to the side. At the start of the battle, that sort of strike would have dislocated the joint. Now, she knew it was merely bruised, not broken, as the man straightened and came right toward her.

She had no shield, no sword. He had both. Her daggers bounced harmlessly away, not finding their targets. He even caught one with his sword, shattering the brittle obsidian.

And he kept coming.

His eyes burned with fury and his breath smelled of rotten eggs. A cut ran from his left temple down the side of his face, through his gray and white beard. The emperor's symbol on his chest glowed with a sickening yellow, like a diseased flower.

Nadeem tried to sweep his feet out from under him, but he hopped over her leg. At least that brought him close enough that she could bash him in the face.

He laughed at her, though his broken nose now poured blood. He licked at it, turning his teeth red and his breath more foul.

Nadeem blocked his next strike with her arm, then whirled, aiming for his head. He ducked.

Damn it! She was growing too slow.

Would this be her failed trial? The one that sent her to the golden court?

A loud growl came from behind her.

Nadeem spun with her next blow, unable to just look.

Riyune stood there. Like the soldier, the dog's mouth was covered in blood, even his teeth.

He growled again.

The soldier fought on as if he didn't hear or see the dog.

Nadeem stepped to the side as the soldier struck out first with his shield, trying to bash her, then with his sword, stabbing at her. He turned to follow her.

Riyune attacked.

He jumped in the air—an impossible height for a regular dog—firmly landing on the soldier's shoulders with all his weight. The soldier dropped flat on his face with a loud, "Oof."

Nadeem danced forward, kicking the man's head. She heard a loud *crack* when her foot connected.

Oops. She hadn't meant to kill him, just to knock him unconscious, so the desert people who were injured could then strip off his armor.

Maybe he'd made her angry, except she didn't feel anger. Or fear. Or any of those emotions that would tie her to this world again.

Just death.

She still took a deep breath. Maybe she did feel relief. She looked out over the other fights still going on at the foot of the path leading from Egreliki. More soldiers were bunched together, leaping down the rocks to join the battle.

"Thank you," Nadeem told Riyune. She took another deep breath.

There were too many soldiers, still pouring down. Had yet another ship docked at the nearby port? How could they stop them all?

Riyune seemed to be having the same thoughts. He looked at the soldiers, then back at Nadeem, his head cocked quizzically to the side.

"We need to stop them at the source," Nadeem said.

Riyune took a step closer to her, putting his back in arm's reach. Then he looked up at her and gave her a doggy grin, as if he found this fun.

"Let's go get them," Nadeem said, trusting that Riyune would understand and carry her to where the soldiers gathered.

She reached out her hand, touching his silken fur, the heat exploding through her as they raced away.

<hr>

Nadeem had been correct. There were more ships. At least two more, waiting their turn, crawling with soldiers like angry anthills. The ships were long, with a broad deck and two masts for sails. Over three hundred men at least waited their turn for battle in each ship.

The ships already docked were still emptying their cargo of men. The soldiers quick marched four across from the pier up the main market trail, heading across the foothills toward Egreliki.

Nadeem didn't know the name of this port town. Not much was here. But someone should have realized that the reason this place was chosen was because of how close it was to the desert. The emperor could keep pouring more and more men through this gap into the desert.

The mass of soldiers sent a tingle of fear through her. It wasn't enough to wake her fully to the world. She found herself shaking her hands, trying to shake off the emotion.

She felt tired, more tired than she'd ever felt before. Her arms shook though she tried to still them. Her legs felt wobbly, like spring reeds. Sharp spikes of pain pierced her chest from the effort her lungs had been making. The cuts on her arms and legs suddenly added to the cacophony of pain.

She had nothing left to sustain her, except the sun and her will.

Riyune suddenly nosed at one of the bags tied to her wide leather pouch.

Ah! She'd forgotten. With shaking hands she slid the knot loose and stuck her fingers inside.

Warm sand caressed her skin. Suddenly, she saw everything much more clearly, the bouncing waves, the rocking boats, how beautiful the ocean sparkled in the sunlight.

Nadeem couldn't stop these soldiers on her own. Not even with the goddess' embrace and a pocketful of sand.

But she knew who could.

***

From high on the hill overlooking the ocean, Nadeem called the shadow sisters to her. They rose slowly, one at a time, probably finishing whatever personal battles they'd been engaged in before heeding her call.

When as many of the sisters had come as Nadeem could hope for, she pointed down at the pier.

"Stop the invaders," she said simply. "Let none of them come ashore and spoil this sacred land."

Though the nameless town and the pier weren't in Trulliç's territory, it didn't matter. She still felt as though the soldiers desecrated everything they touched.

A wave of happiness, possibly even joy, flowed through the dark sisters. Was it because they had a clear duty? Had they needed more direction?

No, that wasn't it. Barzhat's golden court was deep under her sea. Fighting near the water meant that they'd be closer to her.

If they'd been alive, the shadow sisters might have actually have expressed joy.

Like a spring flood rolling from the top of a mountain, they flowed down the hill, aiming first for the soldiers on the road, then sweeping further down to the pier. The men in their path fell quickly.

Yes, some of the soldiers who were already on the road would reach the desert. And hopefully, their deaths.

But no more would come. The source had been cut off.

How long would the sisters remain? How many of them would survive? Would this be their final dance for Barzhat? Or would the goddess ensure that this pier was always protected, always sending more shades to battle against the emperor?

Questions for later, for that indefinable *after* that Nadeem couldn't let herself think about.

Nadeem sat beside Trulliç at the end of the battle. They were both dirty, bloody, sweaty, and tired. The desert people who'd fought with them weren't in much better shape. The star sisters were the only ones still in motion, tying up soldiers who weren't dead, stripping them all of their armor.

As they cast the leather aside, Trulliç sent winds blowing past them, picking up the breastplates and carrying them far off the coast, sinking them deep in the endless ocean.

Riyune stayed with them. He'd shrunk down to normal size and sat watching the star sisters with great curiosity.

Nadeem knew better than to close her eyes in the warm sunlight. She might never wake up if she did. Her limbs felt heavy, as if Barzhat had tied weights to her wrists, her elbows, even her knees and ankles. Her chest hurt. She knew she'd find massive bruises over her entire body when she got back to Hayalevi.

Soft cloth had been wrapped around her right arm, protecting the long scratch she'd acquired there. She could feel her pulse in her bruised feet, hot and angry. Her fingers felt swollen, and probably were, battered and abused.

Still, if she just sat there any longer, she would possibly never walk again.

With a groan, she forced herself to her feet. Trulliç looked up at her in a daze.

"Stay there," she told him. "I just need to move."

It took a few steps for her legs to stop shaking. The pain in her feet subsided to a dull roar. Every breath hurt her bruised ribs. She opened her mouth and stretched her jaw, not surprised to find that her face hurt too.

Riyune appeared at her side, as if there to help.

"Let's go clean up," she said. That was what it felt like they were doing. Cleaning the sand from the taint of the soldiers. As the soldier's half-naked bodies were piled up, Trulliç sank them far under the earth in unmarked graves, clearing their blood from the sand.

The majority of the cleanup work had started in the center of the battle and worked their way to the right. Nadeem joined the smaller crew on the left.

"Ye got to turn 'em over first," a young man directed as she approached. "Use yer feet, if ya can. Then cut 'em at the shoulders. Like this." He walked over to the nearest corpse.

Nadeem didn't physically take a step back, though she wanted to. The face had been hollowed out by the emperor, when he sucked out the last dregs of the poor man's life. The corpse's eyes were as empty as a dried out skull's. The skin had blackened, as if had been burned from the inside, almost turned to ash.

The rest of the man's body wasn't much better. The skin had turned brittle, flaking off as though it were shale. Whatever muscles the soldier had once had were now shriveled. The leather breastplate, which maintained its shape, looked as though it had been built for a man three times the size of the corpse that remained.

This was the body of the enemy. Not a friend.

Still, Nadeem felt a slight wave of uneasy push its way through her distance.

The young man beside her waited to continue until Nadeem gave him a nod. "They ain't all this way. Some of 'ems worse." He gave a dry cackle, then he showed her his knife.

It was similar to the ones the star sisters used, made out of black obsidian. However, the blade had a curve to the very tip, like a knife used for gutting fish.

"Now, youse have to cut here, and here," the man said, indicating the tops of both soldiers. "These where the leather is weakest." He demonstrating, using the tip of the knife to catch hold of the leather, then sliding it across.

"Sometimes ya got to use your boot on 'em," he added when the second side didn't want to cut apart as easily. He stood with his foot firmly on the man's shoulder as he tugged at the leather with his knife.

When the armor had been severed, Nadeem thought she heard a soft *plop*, like the sound a desert mouse made when she landed.

"Now, don't go picking this stuff up with youse hands," the man added. "Just 'cause it's cut don't mean it won't burn." He held up his other hand. A cloth rag had been wrapped around the base of it. He tugged the rag up over his fingers, then carefully picked up the armor with just the tips of his fingers, holding it well away from his body. "Drop it quickly," he added, doing so as he spoke. "Trulliç can be a might impatient, and it won't do to blow away with the armor youse holding."

That almost made Nadeem smile. She knew that Trulliç wanted to return to Hayalevi, to assure those who'd remained behind that they'd survived. But he would stay to finish the job. Even the old Trulliç would have done that.

The young man watched Nadeem clear the breast plate off the next soldier, making sure she understood the job, before he moved off on his own.

Riyune stayed beside her. Was he protecting her? Or merely curious?

He went to sniff each piece of armor after she'd dropped it. The young man had been right about not touching it—even after just a few moments with her hand protected she could still feel how it burned her flesh.

But Riyune didn't appear to have much of an opinion of the leather pieces she cut away. He just sniffed each then went to sit beside her again, watching her work.

The first few breastplates cut easily, without her having to use her foot. The bodies were all caved in, as if they'd been left in the desert for months and the sun had dried them after the birds had eaten their eyes.

After a dozen or so bodies, Nadeem felt as though she was getting the hang of it, though her tired limbs complained every time she walked to the next body and didn't sit down to rest.

The next soldier groaned as she turned him over. Nadeem took a step back, alert.

Was the man still alive? How could that be? His skin looked as burned at the others.

Then his eyes opened.

No, not *his* eyes, not the eyes of the soldier. Someone, or some*thing*, stared out from the holes that had once held the soldier's eyes. The eyes weren't human, but yellow, like a cat's, burning with unholy fire.

The jaw opened and closed, as if the creature possessing the body were trying to figure out how to make it work. With a rattling wheeze, the chest lifted and filled with air.

"What are you?" Nadeem asked. She had knives in both her hands. Her complaining body put all its issues on hold as the dance of death came closer.

Riyune stood beside her, frozen in place.

The eyes from the body glared out at her, as if judging her too unimportant to answer.

Before the possessed being caused the soldier to rise, Nadeem darted forward and started slicing open one of the shoulders of the breastplate.

"Stop," came a commanding voice.

Nadeem ignored it.

She glanced over her shoulder. Riyune remained where he was, as if caught in stone. The dog didn't even seem to be breathing.

Then she returned to her task. The magic holding the leather together was stronger than any she'd encountered that morning. She felt her blade dulling as she hacked at the shoulder piece, using all her waning strength to attack the leather.

"Stop!" the thing cried out.

"May your dance at Barzhat's court be endless," Nadeem replied as she finally sawed through the first shoulder.

"You'll never win," the corpse grated out, his voice sounding much weaker.

Nadeem snorted. "Neither will you," she said as she started cutting apart the second shoulder piece. "You can cast as many men as you'd like against the rocky shores of the desert. They'll all die. None of them will ever reach Hayalevi. Or the desert heart."

"You'll die too," the voice promised, growing more silky but with all the strength of a whisper.

"Not before we kill you," Nadeem promised, ready to swear a blood oath right there and then.

"I will feast on your bodies," the voice—the emperor?—said.

"You're going to have to find them," Nadeem said as she started cutting apart the second shoulder of the leather breastplate. "Which means leaving your comfortable grave, stepping out into the sunlight, and tasting the sand of the desert."

She didn't know if Aunt Parayat would be pleased or appalled at the words Nadeem directed at what might be the emperor.

The jaw moved again, as if trying to spit, but no saliva was left in the burned out hulk.

"Fine," the voice eventually said. The fire in the eyes started to dim as Nadeem continued cutting apart the leather. "I'll be there at sunrise."

"Should we welcome you like a beggar? Or a dishonest guest?" Nadeem murmured. The stranger who appeared at your door for dinner was always invited in, as too often, the stories told of it being a god or goddess in disguise.

"Look for me as you would your precious Barzhat," the voice rasped. "For I will bring death."

"Looking forward to dancing with you!" Nadeem called in a sing-song voice.

Aunt Parayat would definitely be appalled by Nadeem's casualness. However, Nadeem wasn't sure she really cared. She was still far too removed from her situation to be frightened.

When Nadeem finished cutting through the leather, the lights in the eyes winked out, like a dead star. A ghastly scent rose up, like cabbage rotting in an oasis marsh. Nadeem stepped back, coughing.

A plume of greenish gas rose up from the body. It remained shapeless, hovering over the carcass like a hungry vulture.

Riyune suddenly unfroze. He gave her a sheepish look, as if expecting her to be angry. Then the dog darted forward. He leaped into the air above the corpse, his mouth open wide.

Nadeem heard a great *whooshing* noise.

The dog landed on the other side of the corpse.

The poisonous cloud was gone.

Huh.

She was going to have to remember to tell Trulliç about that.

As well as the emperor's approach.

After she finished cleaning a few more bodies…

<hr>

Nadeem took a step back as Trulliç grew angry.

Maybe she should have come to see him as soon as she'd finished talking with the emperor. It hadn't seemed that important at the time.

Nothing did. Breaking her fast in the morning, winning a battle, threatening the emperor—they all bore the same weight in her world.

At least she'd told him while they were still in Egreliki and not after they'd returned to Hayalevi.

CHAPTER NINE

TRULLIÇ

TRULLIÇ STORMED INTO THE WAR council, still angry that Nadeem hadn't told him immediately about the emperor's "visit." He knew he shouldn't be angry with her. The embrace of the goddess kept her apart from the rest of the world.

Was it keeping her safe? He didn't think so. Not when talking to the emperor himself through a corpse brought so little response.

Then again, it wasn't as if he hadn't been wishing for some sort of numbness himself, or strong drink to take away the images of the last day. The scent of the bodies clung to him: not even a strong desert wind could carry the stench away. He'd never forget the image of Zahra lying in the middle of the path, her shirt torn from her, her neck at an unforgiving angle.

There were too many dead for him to compose poems for each. Though maybe he would try. It would take him until the end of his days and beyond.

Levent. Zahra. The other men and women of his city and the surrounding towns. The star sisters.

And maybe Nadeem.

He worried about her. He wanted to worry more.

But he couldn't.

He had to prepare for the emperor's attack the following morning.

Trulliç let the council talk while he cleaned himself. He'd already healed his own wounds, wishing he could do the same for all his people. He did what he could by easing their hearts, sending the desert peace to their side, and cool breezes to help them sleep.

When he returned to his room, Riyune stood in the center of it, looking puzzled.

"What is it?" Trulliç asked, instantly on guard.

But Riyune just shook his head and ambled away, down the stairs.

Trulliç set a mage light against the ceiling, seeing if there were any extra shadows.

Everything looked normal enough.

Trulliç put on a clean shirt, marveling again that he had clothing that was made for him, that fit him, instead of the hand me downs that he'd had growing up. He wore a darker tunic, made out of solid green, with the thinnest of gold stripes. His pants also fit him well.

The *chafiyek* he wore was dyed gold, embroidered with tiny leaves of green. He knew he could call up a glass mirror, silvered and dark, to study himself, though he wasn't sure he'd see the differences that the others sensed.

He still felt them in himself. Even during all the battles over the last few days, he'd never let his rage have the upper hand. He'd been angry, yes, particularly over some of the deaths. Searing mad at the emperor for attacking. He hadn't lost himself in the swirling emotions, though. He'd kept his head as well as he could and so much better than before.

Could Trulliç battle the *Padisha-i-Ghazi*, the great emperor, and not lose himself? How could he counter the emperor's magic? What other tricks would the emperor pull?

Trulliç shook his head. At least he wasn't alone. It was still a novel feeling for him. He'd been so alone, so isolated, all his years.

He took a deep breath, then let it go. That had been another thing to lay at Atça's feet. The older magician had kept Trulliç isolated so he'd never have support.

Trulliç felt a smile cross his face. Admittedly it was fleeting and shallow, but a smile nonetheless.

Though he might die in the morning, he wouldn't die completely alone. And that was honestly something he was thankful for.

———

"We are all in agreement that the emperor will probably attack just east of Gaadiwala," Aunt Parayat said. "There isn't a village there, but it's in a direct line south of Atayurtkah, the emperor's main city."

Trulliç nodded. That made sense to him. "And where will the second attack come from?" he asked.

Aunt Parayat gave him a smile that made him feel like a student again, as if he'd just answered his teacher's question correctly.

"Here," she said quietly. It was north of Egreliki, where Magnus and the others had first touched the desert.

Trulliç nodded. Any ships that hadn't been able to land at the port near Egreliki would likely go up the coast and pull in there. While there were many more ports down the coast, most of them were several days journey from the port town into the desert. In addition, the route wasn't easy: most crossed the mountains. The trade routes stayed on the coast side of the mountains, not the desert side.

"How many should I send to fight there?" Trulliç asked. Just being in his city had revived him. Plus, getting the grime and blood of the battles off his skin had refreshed him as well.

"We seem to be at odds about that," Aunt Parayat said smoothly. "I say throw everyone who can still fight up there. Including as many star sisters as possible."

"And I think that the majority of the army should be with you," Myrizhah said. "You need protection. Not the nearby towns and villages." The two women glared at each other, one protecting the rest of her sisters, while the other thought of her son.

They all turned to look at Trulliç, even Nadeem, who sat removed from the circle, listening but not interacting.

"I need a small troop with me," Trulliç said. He held up his hand so that they'd let him continue. "Yes, the emperor will be traveling with men, but they're a distraction. They aren't really there to protect him. They're for dealing with nuisances."

"Why would you put so many up near Egreliki?" he asked Aunt

Parayat. He knew she'd reasoned out something, but his tired brain was too exhausted to figure it out.

"If you lose, those people will be able to run," Aunt Parayat said quietly.

Deathly silence gripped the rest of the council.

Of course, they should be planning other outcomes. It only made sense.

Trulliç nodded. "She's right," he said after a moment. "The desert people—they'll continue on in the desert, as always. The emperor will persecute them, but he won't kill them. He needs them to provide the empire with the wealth of the desert, the spices, sweet *meslit* syrup, even the salt he likes."

Seydat and a couple others shook their heads but remained silent. They knew he spoke the truth, though he could tell that they wished he didn't.

"The star sisters deserve a chance to live," Trulliç continued. Then he paused and thought for a moment. "The other star sisters, the one who served the emperor instead of coming here, would they let them live?"

Aunt Parayat shrugged. "There will be some persecutions, as you say. But most will be able to live. If they can escape the desert, they can always lie about being here. Remember, not that many joined us."

Trulliç didn't want to agree with her, or to point out that most of the sisters who had come to fight for him were already dead.

"Later this afternoon, I will send those who wish, to Ishmirli, in the west," Trulliç said. He hadn't fully regained his strength, but there was nothing else he could do. "After the sun sets, I'll set out with a smaller group to the spot where the emperor is most likely to arrive."

"Do you want us to prepare a grand tent? So you can welcome your honored guest?" Seydat asked in a joking tone.

"I'm not sure there's anything I can do to bring that thief respectfully out of the night," Trulliç replied seriously. "Although—a tent may make him behave. At least for a little while."

"No," Nadeem said.

Trulliç turned to look at her, astonished. She'd grown so much more quiet.

She'd also cleaned up, but instead of her usual black star sister outfit, she wore a long, off-white tunic, shapeless, gathered around her waist with her wide leather belt. She wore her *chafiyek* around her neck, the black and blue cloth matching her bruises. She seemed to have recovered physically by arriving in Hayalevi, but her eyes were still haunted.

Probably like Trulliç's were.

"Ever footstep he takes across the sand will give him more power here," she said seriously.

"Why do you say that?" Trulliç asked, curious. "I rule here. The desert is mine."

"But it's part of his empire," Nadeem said. "He's claimed the sands before. He's going to try to do it again. Don't let him."

"I won't," Trulliç said. Sometimes he wasn't sure if he was speaking with Nadeem or if the goddess spoke through her.

"Good," Nadeem said, nodding. She sat back and passively looked at the group again.

"I don't want to leave the desert," Trulliç said. "I lose power when I do. I don't want the emperor to set foot on the sands. What, are we just supposed to battle each other from across the border?"

"No," Seydat said, her voice sounding as if it were far away. "You will take a tent with you. But it won't be an ordinary tent."

Trulliç listened to her plan, nodding in agreement.

The others added some refinements, but in the end, they were all in agreement.

It was time for someone other than the emperor to be devious.

* * *

Trulliç sat, nervous as a new bride, waiting for the emperor. He'd done everything he could to prepare the location.

Scholars agreed that the *Padisha-i-Ghazi* was not a land magician. The more fanciful ones claimed that he was an *every* land magician, able to preform his magic throughout the Tanesh empire.

No one wrote of the magic the emperor did practice, though Trulliç now understood that it had to do with the dead.

However, the war council had all agreed that since the emperor wasn't a land magician, there was a good chance that he could be fooled.

The pavilion that stretched out above Trulliç's head was pure white, about as large as the base of Trulliç's tower, and able to easily hold two dozen men. He didn't bother with any banners. Thick rugs woven out of fine red-and-gold wool covered the dirt ground. Many pillows were strewn across the floor, the best Seydat could find in the market of Hayalevi, in every color, not just green and gold.

The seat of honor sat empty, with the finest pillows piled up there.

A silver tea set sat in the center of the area, with a pot of water boiling over a small fire just behind Trulliç. He willed himself to be calm, taking deep lungfulls of the mint and cinnamon tea. He just had to wait a little longer.

All of the people Trulliç had brought with him were stretched out behind him, a solid line, standing on the far side of the desert border. It made Trulliç nervous to be away from the desert, however, he'd agreed that it would be for the best.

Riyune had stayed with Nadeem, back in the desert. Trulliç didn't blame the dog. Riyune, like Nadeem, was a desert creature. Plus, Riyune deserved the chance to run into the desert if the emperor killed Trulliç outright.

Nadeem hadn't liked being sent back to the line. Despite the distance between them, she'd still wanted to be there to protect Trulliç.

But Trulliç had insisted. He needed to meet with the emperor alone. Though he knew better than to see if they could possibly negotiate a peace, he really needed to be able to study the emperor without any distractions.

Before Trulliç had to kill the *Padisha-i-Ghazi*.

Sunlight breached the dunes to Trulliç's right. The pavilion came with flaps on all sides, instantly changing it from an open area to a shaded one.

Trulliç turned his head toward the rising sun, letting it bake his face for a few moments. He longed to just loll in the sunlight for the day. Maybe go out into the deep desert and bathe in the sand like a lizard, letting the heat refresh his blood, heal his body. He still felt stretched thin. He knew he'd been doing too much magic with too little rest.

Only one more hour to get through. Then he would either be able to relax, or he'd be dancing in Barzhat's court, probably for an eternity for the people he'd killed.

As the heat rose, Trulliç forced himself to stand. While he quite enjoyed the warm sunlight, he doubted that the emperor would as well.

When Trulliç finished lowering the thick canvas on the side of the pavilion facing the sun, he looked forward again.

A dark smudge appeared on the horizon.

Trulliç felt his breath catch. Was that the emperor?

The figures slowly resolved.

A large, two humped camel walked at the head of the line, carrying an enormous man who rode under a parasol, protecting himself from the desert sun. A tall gaunt man walked beside the camel. They moved quickly, more quickly than a normal camel would, though they didn't appear to be running.

Beneath their feet, a cushion of clouds carried them along. That was how they moved so fast. They didn't travel on normal ground. No wonder Trulliç couldn't feel them at all.

Behind the pair stretched a long line of soldiers. Trulliç quickly counted. More men than he'd brought, but at least no star sisters. Or none that he could see. He shouldn't assume they weren't there, either hiding among the men or disguised in some other fashion.

If they'd been on the desert sand, Trulliç would have seen them. He would have felt their footsteps. But they were here, on the border, and Trulliç stood on the emperor's side.

The camel, its rider, and the groom strode closer. The groom's robes were done in the same red and gold as the leather armor of the soldiers. But the groom held no shield, and his sword was tied to his back.

Still, Trulliç couldn't dismiss the man as harmless. He worked for the emperor, despite his dark coloring proclaiming him as a desert person.

The man riding the camel had dipped his parasol to the front, so that Trulliç couldn't get a good look at him until he dismounted.

Trulliç took a deep breath and waited patiently, desert winds blowing softly at his back, begging him to return to the sands.

Soon he promised.

He would return to the earth very soon.

The emperor was a tall, *huge* man. He easily stood a head above Trulliç, and Trulliç wasn't short. He was also twice as wide around as Trulliç. His face was full of fat flesh, doubled up on his cheeks and under his chin. No hair grew on his face or his head. He had golden skin without any wrinkles—surely due to magic, as the emperor was at least two hundred years old.

The great cloak of the emperor hung off his shoulders like a dark shroud. Trulliç examined it with fascination. It was made out of row after row of glittering black scales. Were there that many magicians and star sisters? Trulliç had never thought about it before. Or was the cloak made up of scales from both the living and the dead? A thick golden chain held the edges of the cloak at the emperor's neck. The cloak flowed from his broad shoulders down to the ground, like huge black wings.

Trulliç felt revolted by the cloak. Was that because the scales were made out of the afterbirth of a babe with power? Could he fight the emperor in his cloak? Trulliç didn't know.

The emperor didn't wear a shirt under his cloak. His golden skin and fat belly shone in the heat. His pants were made from the finest brown silk that shimmered with red and gold as he walked.

It struck Trulliç as odd that the emperor wore boots instead of sandals, as did some of the merchants Trulliç had met who'd come from Lydae. Wouldn't the emperor want to feel the earth beneath him? Or was this yet another sign that the emperor wasn't a land magician? That he didn't understand the power of the earth?

The emperor's aura was unlike any Trulliç had ever seen. Instead of being solid bands of color, it appeared like a wispy shroud, the colors red and black. It was much smaller than Trulliç had expected, given that the emperor had so much magic.

If Trulliç was honest with himself, the emperor looked like an over-fed baby. Trulliç had never met anyone so fat.

By comparison, Trulliç knew he appeared skeletal. The desert had changed his body, making him more gaunt, his flesh more dry. His skin wasn't soft, but roughened by winds and sand. Trulliç had the same dark coloring as his mother, though his hair was a lighter brown than most, courtesy of his Lydaen father. It still curled slightly when he didn't have it covered with a *chafiyek*.

"Greetings, *Padisha-i-Ghazi*," Trulliç called out as the emperor approached.

He didn't get down on his knees or abase himself on the ground before the emperor.

He did bow his head out of respect, as he would for any leader.

The emperor didn't seem to take offense, though. "Greetings, o king of the desert!" the emperor called out in a high, thin voice that seemed out of place with such a large man.

"Please, come take part in my humble hospitality," Trulliç said, keeping his head lowered as the smell of the emperor passed over him. He stayed frozen for just another moment, fighting his gag reflex.

The emperor reeked of rotting flesh and ashes. He stank as well, as if he'd not bathed in years.

Trulliç willed his eyes not to water as he looked up, finding that the emperor was waiting for him. "I hope that you find my meager offerings palatable," Trulliç said, indicating that the emperor should take the seat of honor.

"No, no, I couldn't possibly," the emperor demurred. He appeared to be studying Trulliç as closely as Trulliç examined him.

"Please, I insist. I know it isn't much, compared to what you're used to," Trulliç said. He found himself relaxing. This was part of the normal dance of life, the offering and refusing of hospitality.

"I wouldn't want to take all that you have," the emperor demurred.

Trulliç made himself keep a straight face instead of replying sarcastically, *I bet.*

After a few more rounds, Trulliç got the emperor settled, and he turned to the task of making tea. An expectant silence grew between them.

"I hadn't anticipated this," the emperor finally admitted. "Though I should have known that you would treat an enemy like an honored guest. You desert people are just strange that way."

Trulliç bit his lips together to keep from replying about how *you desert people* were still going to kill him.

"Hospitality means a lot to my people, yes," Trulliç finally replied as he finished pouring the emperor the first cup of tea.

"You know I can't be poisoned, right?" the emperor said as he took the cup.

Trulliç looked truly horrified. "Why would I do that?" he said. "I would never—that would be rude!"

The emperor chuckled. "Yes, I should have expected that as well. That you'd never poison a guest, even one you meant to kill later. You'd never abuse your precious laws of hospitality that way." He took a sip of tea. "That is quite soothing," he said.

Trulliç looked at the emperor curiously. "Where did your journeys start? Since you aren't of the desert people?" He doubted the emperor was from Lydae, though he did have a large enough nose for it, and the people from Lydae were notoriously tall.

"I was born in the Tanesh Empire, well, back before there was such a thing. Before I conquered all the lands," the emperor said, chuckling. "East of Atayurtkah, along the main trade route with Uluborlu."

"And your family?" Trulliç asked. He'd never known any of the histories to record such a thing. The emperor was always presented as timeless, and the times before the emperor as mere chaos and not worth learning about.

"Rug makers, actually," the emperor admitted. "We would have traded well for such a rug as this."

"Thank you," Trulliç said. "I will be certain to tell Seydat that."

"Your wife?" the emperor guessed.

"I have no wife, no children," Trulliç said. He didn't want to hide from the emperor, to give his enemy a possible lever to use against him.

He got a wide smile in return. "I have no wife or children either. Just a large empire to control. You have no idea how much work that takes, how much effort."

Trulliç shrugged. He was starting to get an idea how much work something like that was. Since founding Hayalevi, he'd had more people coming into the city every day. He'd had to raise houses for them, widen streets, build more fountains.

"Particularly when an upstart such as yourself comes along," the emperor continued. "Tell me, Trulliç, what am I going to do with you?"

Trulliç blinked, surprised. He'd assumed that the emperor wouldn't want to bring their conflict up. Then he realized that discussing business always came at the end of the meal, another part of the desert hospitality. Make sure your guest is fed first and feeling comfortable before you approached the hard topics.

"Let me have the desert," Trulliç said earnestly. "It's all I want. All I need. I don't need any of the rest of your territory. You would still be the emperor over everything else."

"But you see, that's the rub," the emperor said. He looked very sincere, his fat face solemn. "I already own the Qaenev desert. It's mine, and as much a part of my empire as the Kingdom of Lydae. You can't have it."

"It isn't yours," Trulliç contested. "It doesn't respond to your footsteps. It doesn't carry your name to the people there. You don't share their dreams."

"Are you sure?" the emperor asked. "Because I dare say it would, once I set foot there again. Why else would you meet me here, on these lands? Other than to deny my rightful place on your precious sands?"

The emperor kept his tone silky smooth, but his words had hard edges on them, digging at Trulliç.

Trulliç nodded to the emperor. He kept his own tone light as well. "The reason I didn't want you to set even a single foot in the desert is because you corrupt everything you touch."

"Really, is that how you feel?" the emperor asked. He seemed delighted rather than angry.

"I do," Trulliç said. "Seydat has instructions to burn everything from this meeting, including melting down the tea service. Nothing else will remove the taint."

"Wonderful!" the emperor said, clapping his hands, reminding Trulliç once again of a fat baby. "Wonderful. It's so refreshing to talk with someone who actually speaks their mind. I may have to pay one of my servants at the court to do so some days."

"I'm glad my hospitality meets with your approval," Trulliç said dryly. He knew he'd never have that worry—the people of the desert would be honest with him. It was part of their nature, part of his own. If you didn't honestly face the sands, the deceit would kill you, eventually. Mirages were deadly.

"Then, could you do one more thing for me, dear boy?" the emperor asked. He leaned closer to Trulliç, as if about to speak a great secret.

Trulliç didn't recoil, though he dearly wanted to. That stench the emperor carried with him was overwhelming when he drew close.

"If it is in my power to give an honored guest, I will," Trulliç said. That was all the rules of hospitality demanded. Nothing more.

"Could you try to attack me?" the emperor said. "I mean, it's been so long since any land magician was foolish enough to throw himself at my cloak. I'm wondering if it's lost its effectiveness."

Trulliç tilted his head to one side as he considered his options. Was that part of the disgusting smell the emperor had? Was it just the cloak turning him away?

No, the emperor's flesh really was that corrupt.

Then Trulliç turned his attention to the cloak. It didn't draw him in or repel him. "How is the cloak supposed to work?" he asked the emperor.

"You know, that's a remarkably intelligent question," the emperor said with a wide grin. "It's the same reaction that you would have, if you'd had a child. Your magic recognizes the relationship, and won't let you attack."

Trulliç nodded. Few magicians had children, but Atça had told him that if they did, they couldn't use their magic on them.

It was one of the reasons why Atça had been able to strike Trulliç on occasion, until Trulliç grew too large to be smacked easily.

By Atça, at any rate. Myrizhah still had that right. And if Nadeem ever came back, she probably would as well.

"So it's just my magic that can't get through?" Trulliç asked.

"My boy, if you think you can skewer me with a plain knife, go right ahead," the emperor said. He pulled back his cloak along the sides and bared his fat belly.

"Do you mind?" Trulliç asked, pulling out the small bag he always carried with him, filled with enchanted sand.

"No! Not at all!" the emperor said. "Fascinating. You know that land boxes are forbidden, right?"

Trulliç shrugged. "It isn't a land box," he said seriously. "This is just sand. My sand."

The emperor blinked. For a brief moment, worry crossed his face. Then his broad smile came back, bigger than before. "Your sand. Of course, of course."

Trulliç knew the emperor didn't really understand. He wasn't a land magician. He couldn't feel the earth beneath him. He'd forbidden the showy pieces of magic, like a box.

He'd forgotten that magic infused every tiny grain of sand.

Trulliç drew out a handful of sand, lifted it up, then blew it toward the emperor.

He'd killed more than a half-dozen men that way, his sands swirling and choking them to death.

Atça had merely been the first.

The sand flew directly at the emperor's face. Then, as if it, too, was repelled by his rank odor, it turned away.

For a brief moment, Trulliç felt a spike of panic. Would the sand turn and attack him now? How could he combat his own land?

But the sand merely fanned out, then slid away, heading back to the desert from where it had come.

"Fascinating!" the emperor said, "absolutely fascinating! Thank you so much! I haven't had that close of an encounter for decades." He beamed at Trulliç. "It's also good to know that the cloak continues to perform it should."

"You're welcome," Trulliç said. He stood up, stretching. "But now it is time for my honored guest to be on his way back home."

"Oh, no, I wouldn't dream of it!" the emperor said. "Now is the time for you to die."

Trulliç found himself frozen in place. He couldn't move his feet forward or back. He couldn't even wiggle a pinky. He could barely breathe, his chest frozen as well. Ice filled his veins. Pain radiated out with every heartbeat. The smell of long rotted corpses floated over him.

The emperor floated up from his position on the floor, instead of forcing his extraordinary weight up. He threw a look of pity at Trulliç before finally finding his feet.

"You see, while you were offering me your *hospitality*, and really, such a poor thing as this barely rates the name, I was finding your true self," the emperor explained. "It isn't that hard to do. While it's true I don't have *land* magic, as all you magicians pride yourself on, I do have *people* magic. Which is much stronger in the end."

Trulliç struggled to speak. The words came slowly, drawn out, as he forced his mouth to move. "You're...wrong." Trulliç found his senses moved at a snail's pace as well. Still he forced them down, under the layers of dirt at his feet, down under the rocks there as well.

"Wrong? Wrong? My dear boy, look at us here. I'm still hale and hearty, after you tried what I believe to be one of your best attacks on me, and you're here trussed up like the goose for a feast!" The emperor shook his head and walked all the way around Trulliç. "I don't think you're in a position to call me wrong."

"People…aren't…anything…without…land," Trulliç managed to get out. "Without…home." He continued to drive down, down, down, like a seagull plummeting from the cliffs into the ocean.

"You're mad, you know," the emperor said. "I plan on bringing all the prisoners from Lydae down to the desert. They'll be happy to settle here. The desert rats you're so fond of will have to just get used to living in the mountains. With snow."

If Trulliç could have shivered, he would have. Myrizhah had explained snow to him. So had Atça. It sounded awful.

Still, he continued. "Home…is…important. More than you know." There it was. The desert sand buried deep underneath the ground.

The emperor looked confused. Obviously, no one had ever started to free himself from the grasp of death before.

Trulliç couldn't stamp his foot on the ground as much as he might want to. He couldn't make a strong physical movement to bring his magic up.

The sand still rose, like an unstoppable flood. It pushed the fine rug up and away, toppling the tea service, even quenching the small fire still burning. It brushed against Trulliç's toes, giving him more strength.

It even ran across the tops of the emperor's boots, then surged higher.

The sands did recognize the emperor.

They didn't like him. They couldn't do much to him, but they could hold him.

The sand scrubbed away at the last of the magical ties that held Trulliç frozen, swirling around him like a mini-whirlwind. The emperor looked astonished.

Of course, he didn't look worried. Trulliç was merely a desert magician. What could he do to the *Padisha-i-Ghazi*?

"Attack!" Trulliç shouted as the sands lifted him up from the ground. "Attack!

The emperor stayed where he was, sinking in the ever rising sand. His eyes grew wide as he tried to move away and realized he couldn't.

Fire blasted all around the emperor, glazing the sand with its heat.

Trulliç heated the sand further, then cast it back at the emperor.

"How dare you, boy?" the emperor roared. He sounded angry.

He still wasn't afraid. Not yet.

"You will drown on my shore," Trulliç predicted. "Be carried away by the sand. The desert winds will scour away your stench. You and your kind will never walk here again. It is your turn to die."

"NO!" shouted the emperor. Great winds tore out from him, carrying noxious gas.

Trulliç trusted his own winds to keep him safe as he brought more and more sand up. There was a river of sand running deep underground, from the edge of the Qaenev to where Trulliç had set up his tent.

He'd spent much of the night digging, helped by his people, casting forth a huge tongue of sand, then covering it back up again.

The great cloak of the emperor billowed around him, pushing the sand back. While the entire area filled with piles of sand from below, the emperor kept rising on the heap, instead of falling to the bottom and drowning. Trulliç used his winds to knock the pavilion to the side so that their heads wouldn't strike the canvas.

The emperor shot out gouts of flame and gas, trying to strike Trulliç, the sand, anything. Trulliç's winds protected him, and the sand didn't feel a thing.

From the start, Trulliç knew he'd never be able to rip the cloak from the neck of the emperor. Even if he managed to get that close to the emperor, the cloak's chain would be too strong, the links enforced with magic.

However, the scales were merely sewn on with thread. All the stories about the emperor recounted that.

As Nadeem had pointed out, the creatures of the desert would obey Trulliç if he called them, particularly surrounded by the sands as he was.

It was from them that he'd demanded an attack.

A hawk came shooting out of the sky. It pecked at one of the scales, then took off with it like a magpie with a shiny toy.

Other creatures came to Trulliç's call. The desert mice. Lizards. Vultures. Rabbits. Moles. All types of birds. Even the tiny dogs that lived in burrows under the sand and only came out at night.

One by one, they carried away scales of the great cloak.

The emperor roared and tried to fight them off with his hands, blasting them away with his magic as the sand held him tightly from the waist down.

Trulliç tried to catch the carcasses of those who died, burying them deep in the heart of the desert.

He would honor those tiny deaths as much as the deaths of the people who were surely dying around him, holding back the emperor's men.

Finally, the scale that had come from Trulliç's afterbirth was removed, perhaps by the surprisingly tall ibis that had flown in from the nearest oasis. The sands roared as the emperor's power was suddenly diminished.

Now, Trulliç took a second handful of sand and blew it directly into the emperor's face.

"I would see you die," Trulliç said as the emperor started to choke, "rather than sustain your life any longer, or to try to torment you. You are unnatural. Go to the grave that's been waiting for you, then may you dance an eternity in Barzhat's golden court for all the grievances you inflicted on people."

The emperor's golden skin grew red. His eyes bulged out of his fat cheeks. His tongue turned black and stuck out of his mouth as if seeking air. His fat fists flailed in the air, grasping for something, anything. He pounded his arms against the sand, then found he could no longer move them either.

More poisonous gas leaped up from the emperor, horrible noxious fumes that made Trulliç's eyes water even as the winds blew them away.

Great gooey blobs began to fall from the emperor's flesh as the sand took hold of his chest. They rolled down the pile of sand and started to spread out, like a toxic sickly-yellow moat.

Trulliç found he couldn't clear them away, as they sank deeper into the sand every time he tried to pick them up. Instead, he put hard glass around them, capturing them, like a deadly poison. He'd have to bury these capsules too.

The emperor's mass finally seemed to melt into the sand holding him. It was as if a great stitched together man had bled out all the sand that had been inside him. He stopped moving, and a great sigh filled the area.

Trulliç dared to float a little closer. Was the emperor dead? Or was this just another trick?

Nothing moved, however, when Trulliç sent a small whirlwind down to ruffle the emperor's now flat cheeks. The skin had blackened, looking as desiccated as the corpses the emperor had created. He looked like a slug who'd exploded in the sunlight.

A ragged cry went up all around Trulliç. Some of the soldiers still fought on, but many seemed dazed, their connection with the emperor severed.

With a blubbing noise, the corpse of the *Padisha-i-Ghazi* started to sink into the sand.

Trulliç understood. The heart of the Qaenev wouldn't have such a tainted creature on its shores. The emperor sunk deep and deeper still, past the hidden trails of rock and sand and into the core of the earth herself, never to rise again.

CHAPTER TEN

NADEEM

NADEEM WAS SURPRISED AT HOW far back from Trulliç that Riyune wanted to be, and that he wanted her to come with him. She followed him down the line. He kept pausing and looking over his shoulder at her, as if making sure that she would come.

"What is it?" Nadeem asked as they skipped a few more people down. "Why are you doing this? Are you scared?"

She wasn't sure what Riyune looked like when he was afraid. She'd never seen the dog fearful, she didn't think.

And wasn't he a ghost now, anyway? Even in the dim predawn light he appeared to have his own white glow. What did he have to be frightened of?

"All right, fine, I'll follow you," she said when he stood up again, then looked over his shoulder at her after he'd taken a few more steps. They finally stopped near the end of the line of Trulliç's people, with the pavilion over one hundred yards away.

The star sisters were all more concentrated around the pavilion, intent on protecting Trulliç from the emperor's soldiers. However, Nadeem didn't feel demoted by being so far away from the center of the action. Not exactly. Unlike Trulliç, her wounds hadn't fully healed. Her right arm was still bandaged from the battle the day before. Her feet were one massive bruise. So was her left hand and her ribs. A dull constant ache beat under her skin.

Was Riyune just trying to protect her? Surely he knew that she was completely capable of taking care of herself in a fight, injured or not.

She watched with interest when the emperor came up. It appeared to her as if all his group moved on low white fog, traveling faster than a man could run. It wasn't anywhere near as quick as Trulliç could move, however, it was still quite fast.

The camel the groom led appeared placid enough, not a war camel, which surprised her. Surely the emperor would have creatures ready to take him into battle.

The soldiers spread out in a line that stretched out much farther than the line Nadeem stood in. Plus, they stood at least three deep.

An unevenly matched battle. What else was new?

At least the deception seemed to be working. The emperor really sat down to have tea with Trulliç. Of course, the hospitality of the desert people was renown throughout the empire. It only made sense that Trulliç would offer tea before a battle.

Nadeem stared at the dark figure of the emperor. She couldn't make out much about the *Padisha-i-Ghazi*, except for the general impression that he was extremely tall, as well as round. What would he be like in a fight?

The cloak fascinated her. It was his primary protection. He relied on it keep him safe from the magicians and star sisters. No one could attack the emperor while he wore that coat, no one with power. And like Trulliç, a pure physical attack would be near impossible to slide in under the emperor's magical defenses.

Was that the emperor's primary weakness? Like Trulliç's? That he relied on his magic too much?

Nadeem felt the edge of worry start to gnaw at her when Trulliç stood, then stopped moving. Angry murmurs went up and down the line. Nadeem wasn't standing close enough to anyone else to hear what they were saying.

What was happening? Was all their work to be for naught? Had the emperor already gotten the upper hand? Was he destroying Trulliç?

Nadeem breathed a huge sigh of relief when the sand started spilling out of the ground like an errant geyser and Trulliç was able to move again.

That was the last that Nadeem could pay attention to the pavilion. Then she had her own fight to take care of. The soldiers in front of her weren't ordinary: they were part of the emperor's elite squad. They moved as a unit, attacking ferociously.

Fortunately, that was the only way Nadeem knew how to fight. She gladly stepped into the dance of the goddess, reaching that higher plane where all she knew was blocking, kicking, punching, thrusting.

Riyune helped as well, taking down any soldier who dared to turn his back to the huge dog. His muzzle grew red and the air around Nadeem rang with his constant growls.

After a timeless time, the soldier in front of Nadeem faltered. She slayed him quickly, then turned to the next.

He stood frozen, as did the men on either side of him.

Had Trulliç succeeded? Had he killed the emperor?

Nadeem bashed the first soldier in the head, knocking him down, unconscious. That at least appeared to shake the other three out of their shock. They turned to fight her, but their strength had fled.

So had their fearlessness. When Riyune came rushing in, growling, and attacked the one on the right, the one on the left ran away, leaving the line and heading back into the lands beyond the desert.

Nadeem came out of her dance with her hands and feet bloodied but not as hurt as they'd been the last time. Or maybe she couldn't tell, as everything still just hurt.

The others in the line started cheering loudly. Both the men and women were crying, giving tears to the desert, to Barzhat, for saving their lives.

Nadeem wanted to feel their happiness. She wanted to share in their joy. However, both her exhaustion as well the distance away from the living that the goddess had placed her at made it impossible.

She found herself sitting, with her butt in the desert and her legs stretched out in front of her, her ankles touching the border. She felt it was appropriate for her to sit in that spot, neither here nor there.

The battlefield would need to be cleaned up. Would they have to strip the leather armor from all the soldiers again? Since the emperor was now gone, there might be no need.

Where the pavilion had once stood, a huge mound of sand remained. Rocks were already flying to the area, to protect the hill that was as tall as two men standing on each other's shoulders. It was all that remained of the emperor.

What would Trulliç do now? This wasn't part of his lands. Maybe that was more appropriate, though he might be able to claim it, since he'd directed such a huge river of sand from across the border.

What would Riyune do, now that Trulliç no longer needed so much protection? Now that the emperor was gone? Would he just disappear back into the desert? She glanced around, but she didn't see the dog anywhere.

Nadeem felt as though something else was missing. Something else she needed to think about.

Finally, the question occurred to her.

What was *she* going to do, now that it was after the war?

***

As it turned out, they did need to "clean up" the battlefield. The emperor's symbol on the breast plates of the dead soldiers started to ooze a yellowish slime that, according to Trulliç, was toxic magic. They had to use the same precautions and not touch it.

Nadeem worked beside the others, slicing away the leather armor. At least this time, it cut like normal leather, so the work went faster. The sun burned down hot on her head, though it was still early, before mid-day. Trulliç had raised a burbling stream of water so people could refresh themselves, as well as clear off some of the dried blood.

The woman working beside Nadeem accidentally brushed her hand across the yellow goo and promptly started to scream as her hand burned. She was a young girl, not much older than Nadeem's twenty years. She wore a man's shirt, ragged with many patched holes, and hand-me-down brown pants that were tied around her waist with a rope. Her *chafiyek*, however, was new, beige with green and gold stripes, the ends of it decorated with tiny glass beads. Nadeem vaguely recalled seeing her fight: she spat and hissed like a cat, and was very effective with the short dagger she carried. She'd joked about using on her older brothers, once.

Nadeem rushed over to the woman's side, grabbed her hand, then pushed the edge that burned down into the sand. She understood the sand would help neutralize the toxins.

"Trulliç!" Nadeem shouted.

The desert magician appeared instantly at her side. He lifted the woman's hand slightly above the ground, then poured more sand on it, a steady stream. The remains of the sticky yellow goo dripped off and were instantly swirled away by Trulliç's winds.

"That should be the last of it," Trulliç said as he gently rubbed a finger over the back of the woman's hand.

"Thank you," she whispered in a choked voice, her face still wet with tears.

"No, I should be thanking you for doing this dangerous work," Trulliç said. "And for fighting with me."

She gave him a crooked smile. "It was the right thing to do," she said honestly.

One of the star sisters came up and led the woman away. Nadeem knew that her hand would be bandaged and she would be well taken care of.

"Hi," Trulliç said to Nadeem, sounding shy.

She looked at him quizzically. Then she blinked, remembering.

This was after the war.

What was she going to do? How was she going to come back?

"Hi," she said. "I…I—"

Suddenly, Riyune appeared next to Trulliç. He glanced from Trulliç to Nadeem, then sat down on his butt, put his nose in the air, and issued a great, long howl.

The slightest tinge of fear raced through Nadeem. Riyune had *never* made a sound like that. Never.

He'd disappeared after the emperor had died, at the end of the battle. Where had he been? And why was he howling like that?

Trulliç appeared just as bewildered. Then he stiffened, stood, and looked north, out beyond the edge of the desert.

"Something's coming," Trulliç said quietly. Then he shouted, "Everyone! Get behind the boarder! Something's coming!"

Trulliç's people had never strayed that far from the edge of the desert, still, they all scurried across, making sure they were well and truly in the Qaenev so that Trulliç might be able to protect them from whatever it was that came.

For a fleeting moment, Nadeem thought about stubbornly staying on the exact border herself. Then she shook her head. Why would she do that? Was it just so she could feel something? Fear, perhaps?

It took a little while before Nadeem was able to see what Trulliç had been feeling. Large shapes appeared on the horizon, moving quickly toward them. Running. Four legs. Heads pointed directly at them while their hind legs moved the spine up and down.

The creatures shrank as they got closer, changing from the size of a large hut down to the size of a camel, then finally, to the size of a dog.

Blood hounds. Five of them.

They crossed into the desert without raising Trulliç's defenses at the border. Nadeem heard the sigh of relief as everyone else noted that the glass balls remained hidden under the sand. That indicated that either the hounds meant no harm.

She didn't like to think about the possibility that their magic was so strong they just overwhelmed Trulliç's defenses.

They continued their sprint, rushing straight at Trulliç.

No. They split, running around Trulliç and continuing straight to Riyune, who finally stopped howling.

None of the dogs seemed winded by their strange flight. They didn't pant. Their short red-brown fur glistened in the bright sunlight. They didn't smell like dogs either, Nadeem decided. Instead, they smelled like baked dirt and old stone.

One by one, the dogs walked forward and silently touched noses with Riyune. Then sat down to wait in a line beside him.

Nadeem could see the resemblance now. The heads were different—Riyune had different coloring, ears, and muzzle—but the bodies were similarly shaped, with a large chest, a long spine, and powerful hind legs.

When the last finished his greeting, for Nadeem couldn't think of the action as being anything else, Riyune didn't join the others in a line. Instead, he lay down in front of Trulliç, legs straight out in front of him, hind legs curled under.

What did he want? Everyone knew that the blood hounds had been conjured by the emperor. Shouldn't they have just vanished? That was what the war council had speculated.

The dog laying in front of Trulliç grew motionless, as still as a statue. The short, red-brown fur rippled across his back, changing to an ash-white color. Deep inside his chest, the dog trembled.

Fog seeped from the edges of the dog, making it hard to see. Trulliç took a step back, and he called a cackling ball of pure energy into his palm, holding it ready.

A loud *crack* echoed across the sand, like the sound of a spine, breaking.

Nadeem felt herself take a quiet gasp when the figure of the dog *changed.*

The back of the dog rose and rose. Ash poured off the body, making a sound like shifting sand. The smell of sweet incense floated through the air.

The fog cleared away. A man stood there now. He was shorter than Trulliç, with black curly hair, dark skin and eyes, and a proudly hooked nose. He wore a loose shirt and pants, both the same reddish-brown color as the blood hound's fur.

"I am Nishal," the man announced, his voice deep and rough. "I was —I am—one of those who you refer to as the old kings."

***

Nadeem watched with wonder as the dogs, one by one, changed back into men, some old, some young, but none of them ancient. The survivors from the battle stood in an awestruck circle around them as these legends came back to life.

Riyune went last. Nadeem wasn't surprised when he turned out to be the oldest of the kings. He also appeared to be a man from Lydae, with pale skin. His hair was golden white and his eyes were searing blue. While he was about the same height as Trulliç, he was thin and wiry.

He gave her a smile and a wink.

"We knew you could do it," Riyune said to Trulliç as he stepped away from the pile of ashes that had contained his true form. "Well, at least I had faith in you. Even though you were being such an idiot early on."

Nadeem blinked, surprised. Why would Riyune bring that up? All the old kings laughed. The sound grated on her. She wasn't sure why.

"What happened to you?" Trulliç asked.

Of course, the poet would want to know the history behind the kings. Even at her distance, Nadeem knew that wasn't the right question to ask. Maybe it was her training as a star sister that had taught her to not trust as easily.

But the six kings had once ruled the desert from their grand city of Osmerli. In fact, they'd ruled much of the Tanesh Empire before the emperor had come into power.

What did they plan on ruling now?

***

"Before the emperor, there was no thing as a land magician," Riyune said. "Magic was spread out. More people could do small magics."

Everyone surrounding the old kings gasped. No land magicians? More people had magic?

"Women were more capable at illusions," Riyune continued. "While men had stronger physical magic, to match their physical strength."

"And the star sisters?" Nadeem had to ask. "They weren't marked, were they?"

"They were not," Riyune confirmed. He nodded at her, as if he'd expected the question. "They still existed in small, secretive groups that always went around with their faces covered. You never knew if the woman standing beside you truly looked how she presented or not."

The star sisters in the crowd grew still, as shocked as Nadeem had been.

"That was one of the main reasons why the emperor created us," Riyune said. "His original plan was for us to kill any babe of power soon after they were born. But even though he controlled us, that sort of killing weakened the spell he'd put on us. It was so foreign to our natures to kill innocent children. That was when he invented his cloak. By making us protect pregnant mothers, he made the spell holding us stronger."

"And the star sisters?" Nadeem said.

Riyune nodded. "Yes. Even with the cloak, they'd gotten the closest to assassinating him more than once. That was when he introduced the ritual of carving a star into the cheek of a star sister at her coming of age ritual. So that a woman could never completely disguise herself and get that close to killing him again."

Nadeem couldn't help but shiver. The emperor had corrupted their most closely held rituals. By the time Nadeem was born, the star sisters considered the ceremony their own. When it never had been.

"How did he come to power?" Trulliç asked.

Nadeem could tell that he wished he had a scribe with him, to write down all of these stories, probably so he could cast them into poems someday. It made her both smile and shake her head at him.

"The six kings ruled over much of what became known as the Tanesh Empire. You know, that was his original name, right? Tanil. But he erased his name, became just, 'the emperor', as if he was the only one and that there would never be another."

Trulliç nodded as if he understood that already, how important the names of things were. Nadeem knew she'd never considered it. Then again, she wasn't a poet.

"I was a king of Lydae, while the other kings ruled the other parts of the land. We were loosely consolidated, each country with its own character, its own people and problems. Once a year, the six kings gathered in Osmerli, to celebrate our peoples, to talk together, to make plans for the following year, share resources and wisdom." Riyune sighed.

Nadeem could tell that the memory was painful for Riyune.

"Tanil had already become a minor warlord to the east, near the border with Uluborlu. We'd agreed to bring him to Osmerli so that we could negotiate with him, see if we could give him enough land to make him stop warring. While we had guards and soldiers, none of us had a large army. We weren't intent on conquering more people. Our neighboring nations traded freely with us."

Nadeem wasn't sure why she doubted what Riyune said. Maybe because she'd only lived during the reign of the emperor. There were no records, no poems or songs, but she didn't believe that everything was all sweetness and light in the times of the old kings.

"He came with a small group of elite soldiers. Behind him marched a huge army. Remember, there were no land magicians. We had no warning that they were coming. The emperor hid their steps from us."

Trulliç sighed. Nadeem knew he was still upset how the emperor had managed to hide his soldiers from him as well.

"Tyranel agreed to everything we suggested, bargaining hard for a few things, letting some things go. We kings congratulated each other for doing so well."

All the other kings looked angry.

"But Tyranel had tricked us into lowering our guards with him. Instead, he stole our wills from us with his magic, forced us into our hound forms, then attacked the city."

A sigh went through the former kings, some of their anger replaced with great sorrow.

Nadeem could only imagine the havoc the emperor raised on a defenseless population. He would have killed everyone who didn't flee, then chased the ones he didn't catch right away and slaughter them as well. Everyone knew how the emperor treated the enemy, that he never took prisoners, but instead, took their lives for his own.

"We didn't understand the nature of his magic at first. None of us knew that he lived on death. It wasn't a power granted to any other, as far as we could tell. He was unique. While he gave thanks to the gods as one should, it was perfunctory. He worshiped only himself, and power."

The people surrounding the old kings gave a sigh. They'd been taught that the emperor was always right, to give him praise. The rules about always thanking him at every meal were new, but few had questioned it. The emperor would take care of them.

Would they mourn the passing of the emperor? Nadeem supposed a few would. They didn't understand the evil of the man.

Maybe that was why Trulliç had left the large pile of sand, now covered with thick stones, at the edge of the desert. So that people would have a grave to visit.

"We tried many different plans over the decades to overthrow the emperor," Riyune said. "We finally understood that a desert magician would be our best hope, as the sands had never fully forgiven the emperor for his attack. They obeyed him, but very grudgingly. It took the death of thousands for him to have the power to force the sands to cover over Osmerli. It took him years to obliterate the city."

While the other people listening gasped, Nadeem just shook her head and sighed. She remembered Trulliç speculating that just because there were no poems about a great war, didn't mean that the emperor had had the power to kill the kings in a single battle.

"There were many desert magicians over the decades," Riyune said. "All of them died before they could come to full power, either killed by the emperor when he realized what exactly the child could do, or else overwhelmed by the desert itself the first time they walked the lands."

He speared Trulliç with a look. "It was with great luck that your mother bore you so far north. The emperor wasn't really looking in Lydae for a desert magician. Then, you had your great journey here, always moving. The emperor lost track of you."

"Were you the blood hound who accompanied my mother?" Trulliç asked. "The one who changed the tin horseshoe to glass?"

"I was," Riyune said with a lopsided grin. It was a very doggy expression. "Slid the glass into your chubby hand, right after you were born."

"Was Atça part of your plan?" Trulliç asked, holding himself very still.

Nadeem knew that while Trulliç controlled his anger so much better now, his rage at his former mentor would never completely disappear.

"No, that just worked out well for us," Riyune said. "He kept you hidden, better than we could have. We left you with him. He didn't report your powers to the emperor until the very end."

Nadeem bit her lips together, though she wanted to say something, anything, to comfort Trulliç. It was difficult for him to hear that his hated mentor may have saved his life.

At least that appeared to get Trulliç to start thinking.

"So what will you do now?" Trulliç said, finally asking the question that Nadeem may have started with.

Riyune blinked, as if the question surprised him. "Do? We intend to rule again. As we did before."

Quiet engulfed all the people standing and listening. Nadeem saw them all tense. Were they going to run backwards, away from the fight that was about to start? Or would they run forward, to try to protect their desert magician?

"No," Trulliç said. Though the word was spoken quietly, it carried great weight. "The desert is mine."

Riyune laughed. It wasn't a pleasant sound. "We gave it to you, boy. We can take it back."

Trulliç shook his head. "You may have given me the power at the beginning. But the desert has given herself to me. You cannot take the land away from a land magician."

What Trulliç didn't say, but what Nadeem heard anyway, was that

Trulliç would die without the land, starve like a man without food or water.

"Are you sure?" Riyune asked slyly.

Nadeem watched in horror as Trulliç's color faded. The familiar sand beneath her feet suddenly felt as foreign as the rocks and dirt beyond the border.

"You will stop," Trulliç commanded them. Great balls of glass suddenly rose up out of the sand, surrounding the old kings.

"You can't make us," Riyune said. He sounded please, like an older child taunting a younger one.

Yes, the old kings may have had great wealth in their kingdom, and possibly there had been peaceful trade between them and the other kingdoms.

More likely, though, they always held the threat of invasion over the heads of their neighbors. And the terms of their trade would always favor the kings. The other nations were more like slave nations.

Winds suddenly tore through the area. The kings looked surprised. Trulliç called up a powerful ball of pure energy to his hands. The sands came back under his control. Nadeem felt herself taking a huge sigh of relief as the nourishing lands supported her again.

The kings looked at each other. They all began to shake themselves, swinging their arms from side to side. Mist covered them as their bodies changed. Nadeem winced at what sounded like bones breaking as the kings transformed back into blood hounds.

Or what Nadeem had always called a blood hound. These creatures looked like blood hounds, but were different. They were larger than a regular dog. Long fangs grew from their upper snouts, a weapon to use bringing down prey. Their paws were much bigger as well, with sharper talons and longer dew claws.

They all focused their attention on Trulliç. He stood his ground.

The one in front—it must be Riyune, though he looked exactly like the other hounds—stamped his paw on the ground, making the sand ripple.

All the comfort slid out of the land again. The ball of magic in Trulliç's hands died. The winds were chased off.

Nadeem heard the word as loudly as Trulliç did, she was certain.

Run.

Why did they want for Trulliç to run? Was it just part of the chase for them? Or did they want him to leave the safety of the star sisters and others who might come to his aid?

Slowly, Trulliç nodded, as if he heard more than what Nadeem had.

"I will be back," Trulliç directed over his shoulder, at Nadeem.

For a moment, their eyes caught. Nadeem felt her heart beating normally in her chest again.

Then her distance from him and the rest of the world reasserted itself.

The war hadn't ended. Not yet.

Trulliç raced away, heading deep for the center of the desert, with the blood hounds hot on his heels.

While the rest of the group gathered together, muttering to themselves about what they'd just seen and heard, Nadeem turned her back on all of them and went to sit on the border again.

Neither here or there. Neither alive nor dead. Waiting still for the war to end.

CHAPTER ELEVEN

TRULLIÇ

TRULLIÇ FLEW ACROSS THE DESERT. He realized that he'd gone faster when he'd been carrying his people to the battle of Egreliki. He wasn't going slower because he was tired, though he was. A deep weariness had settled into his bones after the fight with the emperor, after fending off so much fire and power, absorbing so much of the emperor's poisonous magic.

He traveled more slowly because needed to think as he flew along.

The other kings had all, in one voice, told him to run.

Riyune had added in a quiet whisper, that none of the others could hear, "It's the only way to save your life."

Though the old kings weren't land magicians, they still had great power over the desert, and possibly all the lands. Their magic was different, however.

Trulliç wished that they'd all met under different circumstances, that he could have welcomed them to Hayalevi as honored guests. He longed to hear their stories, learn their history, and sing their poetry. They could have spent a month together, sitting with scribes who recorded their every word, and still Trulliç would have wanted more.

The kings could take the desert from Trulliç, he knew, if they all worked together. He felt it slipping away behind him as the dogs chased him, gathering the land back to themselves. It wasn't as strong of a hold as

Trulliç had as a land magician: with effort, he could recall it to himself. Plus, the land didn't sustain the old kings, support them as it did the desert magician.

However, Trulliç couldn't stop running. The hounds would tear him apart if he did. He couldn't defend himself from them. The desert didn't recognize them as an enemy, particularly not when they were in their blood hound form.

What could he do? Where could he run to? He couldn't get away. They'd chase him up the tallest mountain and across the deepest ocean. The desert was their home, though. He understood that the blood hounds were originally bred from the tiny dogs who lived under the sand. How or why they were created, he didn't know, though he longed to. What ritual did they undergo, to gain the ability to change from man to dog? It wasn't something they were born with, that much Trulliç intuitively understood about the nature of their magic. His forms were wind and sand, but he was a desert magician. A strong enough magician of a copse of woods would be able to take the form of a tree, maybe even one or more of the creatures who lived there.

But that sort of speculation, that his mind naturally turned to, wasn't helping.

Where could he go? How could he stop the old kings? He hadn't prepared anything. Only through elaborate preparations had he been able to kill the emperor.

The satisfaction at ending the corrupt beast of the emperor was tainted now by the blood hounds chasing him.

Riyune believed Trulliç might have a chance, though, if he ran.

For a moment, up ahead, a dark shape loomed. Trulliç thought it was the cavern that led to the myth lands.

The dark spot turned out to be a sole dune, piled up by the winds.

It gave Trulliç an idea, though.

He was at his moment of greatest need, tired, his magic no longer at full strength despite the heat of the sun beating down on him. He was drained after these last few days, full of battles.

"Help!" he called out to the desert itself. "I swore a blood oath to stop the emperor from desecrating the desert. I have fulfilled my promise. Now, I need your aid to stop the old kings from destroying my lands."

Trulliç didn't know what else to call it. He knew the old kings weren't as corrupt as the emperor. But something about them didn't sit easily with him.

If Nadeem had been more of her old self, she probably would have asked about the intentions of the old kings first.

Too late.

"Please!" Trulliç called out. "I beg you. Help me now in my time of greatest need."

In the distance, a dark shape shimmered into existence.

It was the cavern, the one that had aided him during his first manhood journey. The place that was actually a conduit into the myth lands.

Would it allow the old kings inside? Trulliç nearly gave an exhausted giggle when he remembered that there were only places for four sleepers in the cavern. Maybe it wouldn't allow them all to come in? Though since they were in dog form, maybe it would.

It might be a trap as well. There was only one way in and out of the cavern itself.

It didn't feel like a trap, however. The cavern valued integrity. That was why it showed its hidden jewels to all travelers. Though who desecrated the spot would be left to die in the center of the desert without water.

Trulliç directed his flying legs toward the cavern. It still looked as though it was made out of a haphazardly placed heap of rocks, with thin shale covering the top.

However, even as he grew closer, he couldn't see the guard stone just inside the door. Just endless black, like a starless sky.

Cold winds blew out from inside the cavern. They carried the scent of ash and bone. Trulliç couldn't smell the water from the burbling stream the cavern carried.

He still firmly believed that this wasn't a trap. It was still the same cavern.

And it was his only hope.

Without pausing, Trulliç let the darkness swallow him.

Where was the guard stone? Trulliç kept wondering. The cavern was no longer lit at all by the outside. Trulliç had thought that he'd be able to stop running as soon as he entered, but he plunged into the darkness and kept going, never striking a wall.

The cavern seemed endless. It reminded him of the one time he'd walked along one of the hallways in Atça's house, how it had grown dark and closed in on him.

Trulliç tried to call up a mage light. Normally, in the cavern, it was easy to do.

He could barely conjure a small flame in the center of his palm, and it went out as soon as he let go of it.

Where were the blood hounds? Trulliç couldn't hear them behind him. He couldn't hear anything, or really, see anything.

And he was growing tired, more tired than he'd believed was possible.

He slowed, then slowed further, then finally, stopped.

He listened to his own heart thudding hard in his ears. His breath came in harsh pants. The cool air instantly chilled his sweat, causing him to shiver.

Where was he? What was this place? He could barely see his hand in front of his face. Sand covered the floor, but he couldn't see any walls.

Finally, Trulliç turned around.

Though he'd run and run and *run*, the entrance to the cavern stood right behind him. The guard stone was still missing.

Trulliç took two cautious steps toward the doorway.

Stars streamed across the night sky. The sand glittered like broken glass.

It was the myth lands.

If he went out onto those sands, would he be able to come back?

Trulliç didn't know. But he believed that being in the myth lands would put him on more even territory with the old kings, if they'd follow him here. While Trulliç wouldn't have much desert magic here, the old kings wouldn't have much magic either.

Trulliç stepped out onto the cool sands. The myth lands always calmed him, even though this wasn't really his desert.

After Trulliç had taken a few steps, he looked back the way he'd come.

The cavern had already disappeared.

Six blood hounds stood there instead.

Trulliç watched, his fear turning into curiosity as the dogs stepped forward, then hesitated. Each one started to shake his paws, one by one, as if he'd stepped in something sticky.

They shook their heads. Then, one by one, they each transformed back to men.

It seemed that the myth lands wouldn't accept their dog forms, that they needed to be people here. Trulliç remembered how difficult it had been for Nadeem to perform her illusions when they'd come here. He'd had trouble doing his magic as well. The myth lands wanted its visitors to be in their true form.

However, the kings looked different here than they had back in the Qaenev. They no longer wore the same red-brown shirts and pants, clothes that Trulliç imagined had been part of the blood hound spell cast by the emperor.

Instead, they wore what Trulliç would call kingly garb. Even in the dim starlight they sparkled. Riyune's was particularly fine, with a gold silk shirt, wide green pants, solid leather boots, and a long, black-velvet sleeveless vest that flowed down to his ankles. A thin silver circlet sat on his head.

As they stepped forward, Trulliç gulped. He held himself very still, though his first instinct was to run again, far away and very fast. He shook himself and stood firm.

The creatures who approached him weren't men. Or rather, were no longer men. Instead, they looked like skeletons with skin tightly stretched over the bones. They had stringy hair, and the jeweled rings they wore hung loosely on their fingers. They walked forward awkwardly, as if their joints ground against each other.

What had happened to the kings? Or was this just their true form?

"You cannot escape," Riyune assured Trulliç. "We will destroy you here. You can haunt these lands forever."

Trulliç shook his head. "What happened to you?" he asked. He couldn't help himself.

Riyune gave a wheezy laugh. "We are ancient," he said. "Much older than you realize."

"Why else do you think the emperor was able to live as long as he did?" another of the kings said. "He'd stolen our magic from us."

"That was why you could be enslaved for so long," Trulliç said, nodding. "Because you would live that long."

Riyune gave a sharp shrug, the bones of his shoulders moving up and down. "The spells needed to be refreshed now and again. But essentially, yes."

Trulliç looked more carefully at Riyune. He did seem less solid than the others, here in the myth lands. "What happened to you? When you sacrificed yourself to seal the guard stone?"

Riyune barked a laugh. "There were always more than six women who carried babes of power. There were many shadows of us, fulfilling the contract with the emperor."

Trulliç gasped in horror. "Then your sacrifice wasn't real? The guard stone for the desert heart will crack soon?"

Riyune looked surprised, as if he hadn't thought about that. "Maybe," he said slowly. "But maybe not. When we ruled, Forit's temples were places of great honor. The people sacrificed to them regularly, which we think kept the guard stone strong. However, the emperor did away with all of her temples. It was why he was able to break the guard stone, as it was already weakened."

Trulliç nodded. If he survived this, he was going to have to make sure that all of the villages and towns of the desert started to honor Forit, as well as hire more priests and priestesses. Hopefully they would be able to spread the word throughout the former empire.

Trulliç looked at the skeletons in front of him. While they were the ancient kings, and they deserved to be recognized, he couldn't allow them to continue to live. Their old bones needed a rest.

"You must believe me when I tell you that I wish I could speak with you further," Trulliç said. "I would love to share tea with you, listen to your tales, hear about your world and your adventures. But I cannot allow you to leave here. You may not rejoin the land of the living."

The kings shared a look of disbelief. "How are you going to stop us?" Nishal said. He was obviously the youngest of the kings, his face more fleshy than the others. Perhaps he had more power as well.

Trulliç pulled out an obsidian knife. It wasn't Nadeem's, though it had the same weight and feel.

The kings grew still. Surely they weren't afraid that Trulliç thought he could hurt them with this?

Instead, Trulliç drew the blade across his left palm, making sure to cut deeply. The pain shot through his hand, feeling as though he'd stabbed himself. Blood instantly seeped out of the wound.

Trulliç went down on one knee, thrusting his palm against the desert sands. The agony made his eyes water, his arm burn. He breathed through his mouth, two large gulping breathes. Finally, he spoke.

"I swore to protect the desert from the emperor, that I would not allow him to desecrate the sands there. Now, I swear to protect the world from you and your kind. You belong in the myth worlds. I would give up my desert, stay here for all eternity as well, if that is what it takes to keep you here." Trulliç took another deep breath as he rose back up. "You *belong* here," he said again, feeling it more deeply in his bones. "You are creatures of myth and legend. Your time with the living passed, long ago."

The kings growled, sounding more like the hounds they changed into than men.

Trulliç put away his dagger. He hoped that Nadeem would understand. He shaped a curved sword out of pure light. It took effort to make it hold its shape, and Trulliç had so little energy left.

He planted his feet wide and took on a fighting stance, something he'd seen too many of his people do when the soldiers drew near.

"You cannot pass," Trulliç said. He knew that the cavern that led back to the world of men stood somewhere behind him. "You will stay here for eternity. And we will fight for that long if need be."

The kings looked at each other. Glittering swords, shaped of moonlight and bone rose up in their hands.

Trulliç gulped. Of course, it would be six to one. That seemed to be the odds of his life.

Nevertheless, he nodded. Let them come.

He would never let them pass back to the land of the living.

Trulliç swore as he struck yet *another* sword down from the king he faced, and it didn't make any difference. Since the swords were conjured, it didn't matter if Trulliç broke his opponent's sword, or forced it from his opponent's hand. The swords would magically appear again.

At least he'd managed to dispatch two of the kings and only four remained. The first had been a lucky shot: Trulliç had swung wildly as he spun around, and had managed to strike the neck of Nishal, sending his head flying.

Fortunately, the bodies of the kings didn't appear to be able to regrow their heads. The bones had dissolved into ashes. All that had remained was the thin circlet, tarnished and wan.

Was that where their power came from? Trulliç couldn't see it—the kings were too magical all over for him to be able to isolate one part of their magic from the other.

It gave him something to concentrate on, however.

The next king he dispatched, all he did was knock the crown off the king's head. The bones fell immediately, as if the strings that had been attached to them had been cut.

Now, however, the rest of the kings understood their vulnerability. They hung back, protecting themselves.

It made the fight easier, giving Trulliç a little breathing room. Plus, the kings now attacked one by one instead of two or three ganging up on Trulliç at the same time. Did they not trust each other?

Trulliç wished yet again that Nadeem was at his side. Or that they'd had more time before all of this had started, so that Trulliç could have learned better how to fight. He knew the basics, how to punch and block. He'd also picked up a lot of technique over the last few days, with all the battles he'd been in.

It wasn't the same, though, fighting with hands and feet versus using a sword. The reach was different. Trulliç easily bore a dozen cuts from when he'd overreached himself.

He faced another of the kings—his tired brain unable to cough up the name. It was the one with the tall ibis embroidered on the back of his long black robe. Trulliç remembered the ibis being the one who might have killed the emperor by removing the scale that had been created from Trulliç's afterbirth.

The king in front of him moved something like a bird, high on his toes, with long legs. He had a greater reach than Trulliç. He also made a weird bobbing motion with his head, as if trying to make sure it stayed protected, leaning back as he swung in with his sword.

Trulliç wanted to be patient, to study the king and find his vulnerabilities before Trulliç went for a hard attack. He couldn't, though. He was tiring, fast.

With his left hand, Trulliç made a feint, as if about to throw a punch. Then, he pretended to trip and took a few flailing steps.

This brought the bird-like king forward for the kill.

He didn't notice that Trulliç had swept around with his sword arm until far too late.

The king's feet flew out from under him and he landed flat on his back.

Trulliç leaped up and with the flat of his blade, knocked the king's crown off.

He didn't stay to watch the figure disappear. Two of the other kings attacked, one on either side. Trulliç fought them both, turning from one side to the other. He stumbled back, holding onto his own sword while he still landed on his butt. He sat there panting as the two kings strode toward him, menacingly.

Suddenly, Trulliç remembered the pocket of sand that he always carried with him. Would it help revive him here? He hurriedly reached his fingers into it.

Warm sand caressed his fingertips. Pure air filled his lungs. He caught the familiar scent of baking rock. The world took on harder lines and became less dreamlike.

With a roar, Trulliç jumped to his feet. He swung his blade to the right, taking the king there by surprise. With a real man, chopping through a neck was difficult. There were too many muscles and bones. With one of the old kings, however, the head wasn't attached with much of anything, the bones barely held together.

The head of the king toppled off, landing with a soft plop on the desert floor.

As Trulliç came to face the next king, Riyune came up from behind.

Before Trulliç could attack the king, Riyune slid his sword up, catching the silver circlet of his companion and flinging it out into the desert night.

Trulliç blinked, surprised.

Riyune was the last king standing.

He held up his arm with the sword, then opened his hand. The sword disappeared. Then Riyune opened his arms wide, to show that he was unarmed.

Trulliç remembered at the beginning of the battle how Riyune had only attacked with the others, but how he'd also held back. Plus, Riyune had waited while the others had attacked Trulliç in ones and twos.

"Now what?" Trulliç asked, not lowering his own sword.

Riyune gave him a sad smile. "I, too, would love nothing more but to recount my history with you, to spend time reciting the old poems, and telling you of what had been but was no more."

A wave of relief washed over Trulliç. He was glad that his old companion felt that way. He'd always known that Riyune wasn't "his" dog, that Riyune was his own being. But they'd been together for many years. Trulliç had poured his heart out to his dog more than once, particularly when he'd been dealing with Atça.

"We don't have that time, I'm afraid," Riyune said. "The others are dead, finally. I was the first, and I shall be the last."

"What do you mean?" Trulliç asked. He didn't want to have to kill Riyune. Couldn't Riyune just live here, so that Trulliç could come and visit sometimes? Trulliç would need wise councilors in this new world, where the emperor no longer ruled with an iron fist.

"You were right. We belong here, in the myth lands," Riyune said. He started slowly moving his hands back in from where he'd stretched them out. "We passed out of knowledge long ago. The emperor made sure of that. We have no place among the living."

Riyune placed his hands on either side of his head, near his silver circlet.

"Do you have to die?" Trulliç asked, cursing his soft heart and how his eyes were starting to tear up.

Riyune gave him a sad smile. "While I could live for many years here, honestly, it would be too lonely. And the temptation would be too much, for me to come back and to rule." He paused, then added, "When you made the oath to stay here, to give up the desert in order to ensure its safety, I knew I had to make sure the others remained here as well. You've grown up nicely. I think you'll rule as well, if not better, than we would have."

"Thank you," Trulliç said. While he'd never had heard those words from Atça, hearing them from Riyune meant just as much, healing a part of his soul.

Riyune gave a laughing bark. "Though you'll always be a boy in my heart," he said. With a swift movement, he lifted his crown off his head. His eyes grew wide, startled, and suddenly, younger. "I gift this to you," he whispered as the strength left his body and he collapsed.

Trulliç ran to the side of the old king, but all that remained was ash with a few slivers of bone. Tears sprang from his eyes for his old friend and companion, though he knew that they'd never been as close as Trulliç would have liked.

How could they be? Riyune had been planning on taking Trulliç's desert from him from since the very beginning.

Trulliç felt hollow by the time his tears dried. He also felt lighter and more carefree than he had before, possibly for the first time in his life.

The emperor was well and truly dead. The blood hounds were no more. Just memories and ghosts remained.

Winds that Trulliç hadn't felt had blown away all the remains of what had been Riyune while Trulliç had been crying. Only one of the delicate circlets remained, made of tarnished silver wire.

Trulliç slowly reached for it. His fingers felt the magic of it, as though running water flowed over his skin.

He did not put the crown on his head, however. It wasn't for him. And while Riyune had turned out to be an honorable man, Trulliç still felt as though Riyune followed the god Serril, a trickster to the end.

Instead, Trulliç stood, closed his eyes, and announced his intention. "Let me place this on the guard stone for Forit's heart," he said out loud. "Let the ancient magic wrapped in this crown protect the lands forever."

When Trulliç opened his eyes, there in the distance he saw a dark cavern, the twin of the one that had brought him here, with rocks haphazardly piled one on top of another.

However, for this cavern, the great, gray guard stone stood just outside the entrance to the cavern, completely blocking the way.

Dark storm clouds covered the streaming stars, casting the place in a dull light. The stench of old blood filled the area, making Trulliç's stomach queasy. Whatever was trapped in the cavern sickened him.

The knife that had killed Riyune the first time, or a shadow of the dog, still lay undisturbed on the ground in front of the guard stone.

When Trulliç had placed the body of the dog on the stone, using Riyune's sacrifice to close the hole Marius had made, the center of the guard stone had grown cloudy, like a fog patiently hiding whatever lay beneath.

With steady hand, Trulliç lifted up the circlet and pressed it *into* the stone. The circlet resisted at first, sending tendrils of magic dancing up along Trulliç's fingers, around his wrists and arms, wanting to stay with him.

Trulliç pressed the silver more firmly against the stone, unafraid that it would break.

Slowly, the stone gave way, accepting the circle of silver into itself, taking the magic as its own.

When Trulliç stepped back, the cloudy parts of the guard stone had cleared away. The stone itself had grown glossy and black, looking much more solid than it had before, as though it had been carved and polished from a single piece of onyx instead of rough gray stone.

In the center of the guard stone lay a single circle of silver.

No one knew what Forit's symbol had been, before the emperor had destroyed all her temples. Most of the gods and goddesses were represented with straight lines, while Onnet had the shape of a horseshoe.

Maybe Forit's symbol could be a circle, to show her unending love, and how her death led to more life which in turn, always led to more death. The circle always turning, never finished.

Trulliç resolved to create yet another poem, now that the war was truly over.

Night had fallen by the time Trulliç returned to the true desert. The instant he set foot on the sands he knew that the cavern had deposited him close to where he'd first run into it. The sands around him knew his name, but they no longer answered to him, the ties having been broken by the old kings.

Slowly at first, then more quickly, Trulliç gathered the sands back together, bringing all of the desert back to him. The cavern had refreshed him, given him time to sleep and heal, along with delightful water to drink. It had shared more dreams with him this time, showing how the gods had been the ones to build the rocks around Forit's heart, then how the old kings themselves had crafted the cavern, calling a shadow of the original to them, to act as a conduit.

It offered to bury the emperor's staff deep in the myth world for him, along with the deadly yellow poison that had poured off the emperor. Evidently the emperor had melted some of the bodies of the dead, rendered them for their fat, then used it to power his corpulent body.

Trulliç gladly took the cavern up on its offer, knowing that those powers would be safe in the land of the myths.

When Trulliç arrived at the edge of the desert, he found all his people still there, holding vigil. They'd felt the shifting sands when he'd returned, but they wouldn't allow themselves to believe that it was true until they'd seen him.

Trulliç spent more time than he liked reassuring people that the old kings were really gone, as was the emperor. No, he didn't know what was happening in the rest of the empire. He was going to be sure to hear about it, though. He would send out runners in the morning to go fetch the news, heralds telling the tales of the great battles the desert magician had been in, and how the emperor was now dead.

Finally, Trulliç was able to gather his people together and bring them back to the shining star of the desert, his city, Hayalevi.

Nadeem stayed by his side, silent and reserved as always. He didn't know what they were going to do, now that the war was truly over. Surely she'd come back to him? Remove the distance between them?

But Nadeem hadn't recovered by the next day, or the one after that.

It took Trulliç a week of trying different things before he finally knew what he should do.

He was, yet again at the end of his rope, in his hour of need.

So he took Nadeem out into the desert and called the cavern once more.

CHAPTER TWELVE

NADEEM

NADEEM WANTED TO REJOIN THE world. However, she didn't know how. She couldn't pay attention to Trulliç, no matter how much he might dote on her. She wanted to miss Riyune—he'd been there as long as she'd know Trulliç, but she couldn't. She found herself pricking her fingers with the tip of her knife blade, just to make her feel.

When Trulliç saw the blood she drew, he told her it was enough.

But what could he do? The war had ended. He still was the desert magician. Would he be the last of his kind? When the last of the land magicians died, would the magic they held seep back into the earth? What would the world change into, if more people had magic again?

Nadeem didn't know, and though she wanted to be excited about the prospect, felt as though it was just too much effort.

News was slowly trickling into Hayalevi. It would take months, possibly years, before they heard from northern Lydae. But everyone had noticed the blood hounds disappearing. The emperor's symbol had supposedly fallen from buildings with his passing. People dreamed of stars shooting across the sky, usually a sign of great deaths.

Still, Nadeem felt nothing.

She knew about the star sisters calling an emergency meeting of all the *kabils*. The women had a right to know their heritage. Nadeem told them everything she could from her dream that Riyune had given her, of the old kings, how the star sisters went about completely covered, with just their eyes showing so that none knew their faces. They could become anyone they wanted to be.

Would there be more star sisters like her, who chose to mangle the mark on their cheek? Would they change, as she had? Become creatures of the sea, or trees, or even mountains and sand?

She refused to go with them, however. She still belonged here, in the desert.

Though here was still not *here*.

It didn't surprise her when Trulliç asked her to accompany him out to the desert. A tiny thrill went through her, there and gone.

Was he going to try to kill her? Bury her deep in the sands? Free her?

But no, nothing as deadly as that.

He carried them swiftly across the sands. She traveled easily with him, enjoying the night breezes blowing through her short hair, which she hadn't bothered to cut in some time. It was starting to tickle the edges of her ears. She knew before, she would have already been annoyed enough to cut it.

Now, it was just one more thing that might bring her closer to feeling.

A dark shape formed on the horizon. With a quiet gasp, Nadeem realized that Trulliç was taking them toward the cavern.

Did he expect her to find her cure there? Would the waters there soothe her heart, as they had always soothed her skin?

She found herself suddenly curious, poised again on the edge of being alive.

And then hanging there, as always, never able to take those full steps in again.

The cavern seemed much as it always did. The sound of the burbling water soothed her, and the coolness of it indeed, did make her heart feel less heavy. They stretched out and slept on the shelves, with Nadeem up higher than Trulliç. That just felt right, though she knew that she probably no longer needed to defend him.

When she awoke, the stars streamed across the sky, lighting the cavern with an eerie glow.

The last time she'd been here, she'd gone to ask the goddess for a boon.

Was that what Trulliç was about to do?

When Nadeem stepped onto the sands, she suddenly felt the weight in her chest. It had been a part of her for so long that she didn't feel it as separate from herself, but as much a part of her as her bones.

Trulliç let Nadeem lead the way. She did, but didn't, know the direction. Away from Forit's heart, that much she knew. But where had she found the goddess the first time?

Winds carried sweet scents to them as they walked. Trulliç kept lifting his head up and looking around, as if expecting to see someone there, maybe a ghost.

Would the old kings remain to haunt the myth lands? Nadeem hoped not. She wanted them to be dancing in Barzhat's court, able to be reborn again finally. Though they would dance for a long, long while, she knew. Not because they were particularly bad men, but because they'd lived for so long, they were likely to have done many bad deeds over the course of their lives.

Finally, they reached the area that Nadeem knew, the hollowed out spot where the shadow sisters had come to watch her dance. Trulliç appeared to recognize it as well from her description of the place.

Trulliç led Nadeem to the center of the arena, holding her hand tightly. He kissed her temple, tears making his eyes glitter. He squeezed her hand one last time, then he left her there and went to sit on the side of the bowl, to watch.

Nadeem wasn't sure exactly what he expected of her. But the last time she'd been here, she'd danced for the goddess.

She started as she had the first time, her palms pressed together as she bowed her head low to the north. Then she started to dance again, those slow practice steps, blocking, sweeping away legs and arms, punching and kicking. A dance she knew so well.

When she finished, she immediately started again, a flowing river of steps.

Slowly, Nadeem started to speed up. She didn't allow herself to hurry, to rush to the end.

This might be the last time she danced for Trulliç. She needed to give him time to say goodbye.

She kept moving faster, though, until her hands and feet were blurred. She jumped high into the air when she kicked, higher than she'd ever jumped before. Her breath came hard and fast. Her fingers and toes tingled as she danced, the blood pumping hard.

Finally, she felt the teardrop buried deep in her chest start to move. She couldn't resist the temptation to look down.

It was rising out of her skin, like a monstrous growth.

She couldn't afford to stumble. If she did, the goddess might never take back her gift.

Faster now, Nadeem danced with all her heart. She wanted to return to the desert, to really feel the sand beneath her feet again. She danced for the coming dawn, to be able to revel in all its glory. She danced for the coming heat of the sun, how slickly it would make her sweat. She danced for the coolness of the water in the oasis, how it would soothe her burning throat.

She danced as she had never danced before, giving all of her life to the goddess so that she might enjoy this one last bit.

The teardrop in her chest rose up, until just the tip of it was still connected, a single thin piece of skin looped through the top of it.

Nadeem pushed herself to go faster. This was for the goddess she loved, who she would welcome forever at every meal. This was for her shadow sisters, who had protected the docks from the invading soldiers. This was for all the good men and women who had died defeating the emperor.

But Nadeem was only human. She could only push her body so far, though it had accommodated her much further than she'd thought possible.

She faltered in the same place she had the first time, by swinging out her leg then not drawing it back far enough. She didn't land solidly.

The next step, instead of bringing her foot out in front of her, she brought it too close to her first, misplaced leg. She tripped, and had to stumble forward a few jarring feet.

The teardrop hanging from her chest broke free with the last jolt, a searing pain that went straight from her chest to her belly.

Her gift from the goddess dropped onto the sand at her feet, disappearing as it struck the ground.

The world rushed back into Nadeem. She felt everything, her sore feet, the stitch in her side, how her arms trembled and her back sweat. She smelled the sweet scent of incense and desert rock, already tasting the mint tea that Myrizhah would have ready for her. Her eyes cleared and the night became brighter.

At the front of the arena, Nadeem thought she saw the goddess again. Or a shadowy form of her, with two legs and four arms, her black face and her blue face arranged side by side.

Nadeem felt welcomed by the goddess, who seemed pleased to see her, and possibly slightly sad to see her go.

But she would return, she knew.

Everyone, even the old gods died.

The goddess vanished and Nadeem found herself swaying. She collapsed onto her knees, and found herself weeping. All the tears she hadn't shed for the last few days came pouring out of her. She mourned for the all the dead, Riyune included. She mourned for how much she'd hurt herself and Trulliç as well. She mourned for the days she'd lost.

As her tears slowed, she found Trulliç kneeling beside her. He kept himself apart from her, though she could tell how much he longed to take her into his arms, a solid rock who would always be there for her.

And she cried a little more for him as well, leaning against his solid bulk.

When all her tears were spent, Nadeem finally nodded.

"Let's go home."

———

Nadeem stood at the top of Trulliç's tower, leaning against the balcony, looking out over the desert. Stars filled the night sky. She thought she smelled the ocean sometimes on the strong breeze, but the rest of the time, it was just the dust from the nearby hills, the roasted chicken one of the nearby families was cooking, and the warm smell of the nearby palms and dates.

It had been three nights since they'd come back from the lands of myth, since Nadeem had fully returned from the dead.

It was still hard sometimes to be in the land of the living. Nadeem found her senses raw, like a newborn baby. She had raced to her room and cried more often than she ever had in her entire life. Not necessarily by sad things, though the ceremonies they'd had recently to commemorate the dead had certainly counted.

Joyous things made her cry as well, like being with Trulliç in bed, watching the sun rise, seeing a flower bloom in the oasis, or even tasting a sweet fig.

Nadeem had never thought that she'd have a home, not really. She'd believed that she would always be moving, roaming the empire, doing the bidding of the emperor himself as one of the special star sisters. Kardeş would be her main place of operation, where she'd recover between jobs. But it wouldn't truly be a home.

Hayalevi was closer to what she thought about as a home. She had her own building now. Trulliç had raised it for her. It was next to his tower, close to Seydat's house. It had its own bathing room, where she could pump up water and have it shower down on her head. It also had its own cooking hearth, so she could prepare meals.

It wasn't very large, not any bigger than the tent Aunt Parayat stayed in at Kardeş. But Nadeem was already starting to make it hers. A small basket of carded wool and a drop spindle now sat in one corner. Trulliç had already offered to buy her a loom at the market. Her bed had a quilt on it that had been specially made for her, with patterns of stars sewn into it.

Everything Nadeem could have asked for was here. A kind lover who was also her friend, who made her laugh as well as made her think. She could take him in a fair fight, though he was getting better at wrestling.

She had many people to work with, star sisters who were looking for a new path. They did but didn't want to follow hers—she knew that few would completely turn their backs on the sisters as she had.

Then again, few had a broken blood oath in their past.

Still, Nadeem found herself drawn up to the top of Trulliç tower and casting longing eyes at the horizon.

Trulliç came up from behind her. They both wore merely sheets out of courtesy, though Nadeem would have gone naked. Trulliç wanted to approve, but he was still shocked at the core with how free she was with her body.

At least he understood her mood instinctively, that she needed a friend and not a lover. He kissed her bare shoulder but didn't put his hands on her. Instead, he stood next to her, leaning beside her and looking out over the desert.

"Trulliç," Nadeem started. Then she stopped again. She didn't know what exactly she wanted to say, let alone how to say it. "I promised you before that I'd be honest with you."

Trulliç smiled and nodded, but continued to stare out at his desert.

"I'm grateful for everything you've done, everything you've given me. Even the poem's you've composed for me," she added. She'd been delighted when he showed her the start of his first composition, detailing the amazing work that a star sister and a land magician could do when they worked together.

Trulliç nodded again. His smiled grew wider.

"But I need…I need…I don't know what," Nadeem said with a heavy sigh, feeling defeated.

"Do you want me to tell you what I think you need?" Trulliç asked, looking over at her.

Strange. He didn't seem the least bit afraid of talking with her honestly. That was something that Nadeem was truly grateful for. Though she hadn't had that many relationships, no one had ever been as open and honest as Trulliç had been, both about his feelings as well as his own needs.

"I think your feet are telling you to dance away. You thought you'd travel, and now, though you have a comfortable home, it isn't enough."

Nadeem stared at him in astonishment. That was exactly how she felt. "I don't want you to think I'm not grateful for all that you've done for me," she said, wanting to reassure him.

Trulliç gave a short chuckle. "I know you're grateful. I actually had a bet with myself how long it would take you to realize that you needed to go travel for a while. I'm surprised that you lasted this many days."

"Really?" Nadeem asked, surprised.

Trulliç shrugged. "The bet was somewhere between two days and two months," he admitted. "But I knew you'd leave, sooner or later."

Nadeem nodded.

Trulliç reached over and took her hand gently between his. His skin felt rough as always. It was as warm as a rock kissed by the sunlight.

"I also think you'll always come back," he said, stroking the back of her hand with a single finger. "Or at least, that's my hope."

Nadeem smiled at him, her heart feeling lighter. "I will always come back," she promised solemnly. "I am a desert creature, like yourself. Sand swims in my blood, just like it does in yours."

"You know that I would like to travel with you someday," Trulliç said. "But right now…"

"I know. You couldn't possibly leave." The empire was still coming to grips with the death of the emperor. Most places could run themselves, and though the emperor was gone, their daily life hadn't changed that much.

Though they no longer gave thanks at every meal for the emperor. That order had been rescinded. None of villagers Nadeem had talked with seemed to mind.

Still, representatives from the major cities came pouring into Hayalevi every day to meet with the desert magician. Ambassadors and governor's assistants. They met with each other as well, signing new trade agreements, and peace treaties.

There were still barbarians north of Lydae who would threaten her borders. Trulliç had no troops to offer, however. The emperor's soldiers were on their own. Some of them had banded together, offering their services to the larger warlords and kings.

Their magical armor had disintegrated over the weeks, the toxic yellow goo dripping off and needing to be buried.

Many of the soldiers actually were able to go home finally. Towns absorbed the returning brothers and fathers as well as they could.

Some of the coastal towns had actually asked for more soldiers to be sent their way, the ones who wanted to become seamen. There were always rumors that the endless ocean wasn't, in fact, endless, that there were other continents to find and explore.

So Trulliç couldn't leave Hayalevi, not yet. Not while so much still needed to be settled in the new world. Maybe in a year or two, though.

"You don't need my blessing," Trulliç said. "I want you to feel free to come and go as you please."

"Really?" Nadeem asked. She remembered her encounter with Levent, who would have tried to hold onto her with both hands if she'd ever dallied with him again.

"Really," Trulliç said. He took both of her hands in his now. "I want you to be free to fly and dance and fight as you need to. And to return to me, when you will."

"Is that what you want?" Nadeem asked, her heart already singing, plans forming about what sort of pack she'd take, where she'd travel to first.

"Of course not!" Trulliç said, laughing. "I'd always prefer for you to be by my side. But that would kill you, the free spirit inside of you. I'd much rather that you be free and happy, and return to my side willfully, rather than try to trap you and cage you."

Nadeem pulled Trulliç in for a deep kiss of affection. "Thank you," she said, knowing that by setting her free, he'd just captured her heart completely.

"We have all the world, and all the time, to explore these ties between us," Trulliç quoted. "But for now, fly."

Nadeem nodded, settling herself against his chest but still looking out over the desert spread out below them.

In the morning, she'd be gone, only to return to him time and time again, blown there by the desert wind.

GODS AND GODDESSES

Barzhat

The goddess of death lives beneath the great inner sea of the Tanesh empire. She sits in judgment of the dead on her throne encrusted with pearls and shells. In front of her is a huge golden court, full of souls dancing.

Every bad deed a person commits while they are living is weighed by Barzhat after they die. She creates a black vest covered with golden weights, each shaped like a teardrop. You must dance before Barzhat until all the weights fall from the vest. Only then will Barzhat give you the final kiss of true death, cleansing your soul for rebirth.

A common curse: May you dance forever in the goddess' court.

The star sister Manisat picked up an *ağrikat* shell on the shore of the Barzhat Sea. When she raised the shell to her ear, she heard the sad sighs of the goddess Barzhat and realized how lonely the goddess was. Manisat had made her way to the goddess' golden court while she'd still been alive and had promised the goddess that the star sisters wouldn't merely venerate her, but love her. They would welcome the goddess at all their feasts, big and small. A bowl was always left empty at every meal, a welcome place for the goddess.

Barzhat tests the sisters sometimes, coming for dinner as a stranger.

They must show her hospitality or she will make them dance. However, in return for a star sister's devotion, Barzhat will grant her a single boon during her lifetime, if her need is great enough.

Though cutting across the Barzhat Sea would make travel from one end of the empire to the other faster, no one sails across it regularly. Men can only travel on the waters at her indulgence. Sailors must always be on the lookout when in her territory. If the waters are clear and blue, they can travel freely. If the waters turn black, they run. Otherwise, the goddess takes them down into her golden court where they must dance for centuries.

The goddess is always depicted with two faces, one blue and one black. The blue face is used for judgment. The black face is used for death. She is often called fickle, and is temperamental, as are all artists. She is often shown with four dancing legs and twelve arms, each holding a different weapon.

Symbol: Feet. Also represented by a single line toward the bottom of the space, ___

Colors: Blue and Black.

Innis

The god of fertility lives in the court of the gods. He is forever mourning his beautiful wife, Forist, whom he killed in the great battle with the darkness, and from whom all humanity came. He is known as a dark, somber god. Brining a new life into the world isn't to be done lightly.

Symbol: The spear. Represented by a single horizontal line —

Colors: Red

Serrat/Serril

The goddess/god of desolate places lives in the desert.

Like Barzhat, Serrat/Serril has two faces, a female and a male face. The male aspect (Serril) is worshiped by the land magicians, while the female aspect (Serrat) is honored by the star sisters.

Serrat/Serril is known as a trickster god. He/she leads men and caravans astray in the desert by creating fake oases. He/she also tricks sailors by making Barzhat's waters seem calm.

Yet, Serrat/Serril just wants to be loved.

Originally, Serrat/Serril lived in the court of the gods. However, the gods banished the god/goddess after he brought magic to man. Serril, in his male form, made a bet with the goddess Onnet, that a mighty human hunter could out shoot the goddess and her bow. In order for the hunter to win, Serril gave the human magic.

As Serrat, the goddess has a birthmark in the form of a star on her left cheek, which is why the star sisters carve one in theirs. However, she isn't much loved by them. (They love Berzhat instead.)

Symbol: Z

Colors: White (for Serrat) and black (for Serril)

Enkat

The goddess of rain lives in the court of the gods. She dances for the gods and goddess until the sweat pours from her and drips down from her hair to the earth as rain.

In the desert lands, Enkat is often portrayed as a female form with no face, just hair streaming down everywhere.

Symbol: Represented by three vertical lines. | | |

Colors: Brown and green

Xannil

The god of the sun lives in the court of the gods. In the north, Xannil is often portrayed as a fair-haired, happy god. In the south, he's shown as a darker, sullen, sadistic god. He is married to Enket. Stories tell of how jealous he gets. When he's in a rage, he hides her or sends her away so there's no rain. In addition, Xannil is also jealous of Enket's brother, Innis, the god of fertility. They are forever trying to best each other in drinking contests and wrestling matches, often with disastrous results. Serrat/Serril is usually called to come and fix whatever has been broken.

Symbol: Three horizontal lines.

Color: Yellow

Onnet

The goddess of childbirth and the hunt lives in the court of the gods, though she is often away, traveling, hunting.

Onnet is often portrayed as a crone, though she can take the form of a golden goddess as well. She aids women in childbirth and through their pregnancy. She has a magical bow and can shoot down any prey, no matter how far away. She also uses her bow and magical arrows to bring couples together. There are many stories of young men and women who are great hunters and shoot an arrow into the air, vowing to marry the person who finds it, who after many trials does turn out to be their one true love.

Symbol: Omega. Often represented by a horseshoe.

Color: Orange and green

Creation Myth

In the beginning, there were just the gods and goddesses and no light. Darkness reached everywhere. The gods and goddesses fought with each other all the time just to bring some sort of activity to their endless nights.

So Xannil, the god of the sun, created the first light, which the darkness stole away. He created a second light, which the darkness stole again.

After the third light had been stolen, the gods declared war against the darkness. The darkness divided itself into many beings to fight the gods. The battles raged across the heavens for eons.

Forit, Innis' wife and the fairest of the gods, sang such a beautiful song that the darkness revealed its heart. Innis pierced the heart with his great spear, killing the darkness.

However, the only way Forit could draw out the heart of the darkness was by binding it with her own. When Innis killed the heart of the darkness, he killed his own wife as well.

Forit's body fell from the court of the gods and became the earth. Her teeth became the mountains, her fingers became the many rivers, and the place where her heart had been became the desert.

As the gods and goddesses grieved the loss of the fairest of them all, their tears fell on her prone body.

Forit's freckles, the only imperfection about her, became humanity. The darker freckles became the people of the south, the lighter blemishes became the people of the north.

There are some myths that her heart, still bound with the heart of darkness, lives in the center of the desert.

ABOUT THE AUTHOR

Leah Cutter writes page-turning, wildly imaginative fiction in exotic locations, such as a magical New Orleans, the ancient Orient, Hungary, the Oregon coast, rural Kentucky, Seattle, Minneapolis, and many others.

She writes literary, fantasy, mystery, science fiction, and horror fiction. Her short fiction has been published in magazines like *Alfred Hitchcock's Mystery Magazine* and *Talebones*, anthologies like *Fiction River*, and on the web. Her long fiction has been published both by New York publishers as well as small presses.

Find Leah's books here.

Follow her blog at www.LeahCutter.com.

Come someplace new...

If you'd like to be notified of new releases, sign up for my newsletter.

I will never spam you or use your email for nefarious purposes. You can also unsubscribe at any time.

http://www.LeahCutter.com/newsletter/

Reviews

It's true. Reviews help me sell more books. If you've enjoyed this story, please consider leaving a review of it on your favorite site.

ABOUT KNOTTED ROAD PRESS

Knotted Road Press fiction specializes in dynamic writing set in mysterious, exotic locations.

Knotted Road Press non-fiction publishes autobiographies, business books, cookbooks, and how-to books with unique voices.

Knotted Road Press creates DRM-free ebooks as well as high-quality print books for readers around the world.

With authors in a variety of genres including literary, poetry, mystery, fantasy, and science fiction, Knotted Road Press has something for everyone.

Knotted Road Press
www.KnottedRoadPress.com